WINGS
BEYOND RIO

by

J. GORDON ROBINSON

THE CHILDREN'S PRESS
LONDON AND GLASGOW

To " DINTY "

CONTENTS

CHAPTER ONE

DA CUYTA

IF PETER CLINTOCK impressed Pernambuco with his grave courtesy, Dandy Paget took the city by storm. This little man, agile despite his tendency to fat, had caught the local fancy with his first request after the " Thunderbolt " had touched down on the flying field—a cocktail, and after that a smoke.

Record flights do not allow of social contacts at great length, and the flyers had merely been taken by car to the nearest hotel; but in Brazil tongues are the only things human that move fast, and while the flyers slept, Pernambuco talked.

The women especially listened to the story of how Dandy had somehow contrived to shave during the forty long hours he had been jammed in the narrow cockpit of the " Thunderbolt "; how he apologised for the appearance of his clothes, and raised his glass to the Governor's lady with a wry smile after flying all the way from England. That man was notable!

But the men preferred to recall how Peter, stepping from the 'plane, had answered the reporter's inevitable query: " In the first place, I am delighted to set foot once again in Brazil, where I spent so many happy years as a child."

Clintock spoke fluent Portuguese, and understood that in South America flattery is not deceit,
but good manners.

And while Pernambuco talked, Squadron-
Leader Clintock and Flight-Lieutenant Paget
snatched the six precious hours of sleep that their
schedule allowed them. Then eventually it got too
hot and the talkers joined the flyers in repose.

Promptly at two o'clock Clintock, trusting his
schedule to no one, was wakened by the tinkle of
his travelling alarm clock. He woke Dandy, who
silently gathered his bed clothes about his naked
form—record 'planes carry no luggage—and went
in search of the bath.

Bathed and refreshed they struggled into the
clothes they had kicked off on to the floor that
same morning, and descended. At the bottom of
the stairs they ran into the huge negro who was
about to make his way up to call them.

" Thank you," Peter gave him a twenty milreis
note, " but the car is the urgent need of the hour."

The streets were hot and deserted, and once
again Clintock congratulated himself that he had
left the question of food to the American staff at
the flying field. While they ate he nodded briefly
to the series of comments the ground engineer had
to make, and then stood, melon in one hand,
meteorological report in the other, alternately
sucking and frowning as he glanced from the type-
written sheet to the huge map of the American
continent on the wall.

" I can't thank you fellows enough," he said as they started to shake hands all round, " working in the heat of the day for us. Some day perhaps we'll fix up something for you, and—I beg your pardon, senhor."

Turning to leave the wireless room he had run into a tall dark-eyed man, faultlessly dressed in a Palm-beach suit and panama.

" Squadron-Leader Clintock?"

" Your willing servant, senhor."

The man had the clothes and accent of Rio de Janeiro, and in a country twice in a decade on the verge of civil war, the local and the federal authorities sometimes clash. Success with the one will often bring down the wrath of the other. So Peter, with visions of his precious schedule ruined for want of one of the many permissions that tie down international aviation, was the soul of conciliation.

" You are flying to Chile, I believe?"

" Antofagasta, I hope."

" Good. I will give you a quarter of a million milreis* for a passage on your 'plane. I am in a hurry."

Clintock turned, partly to take a sheaf of papers from Dandy, who had just come up, partly to hide his astonishment.

" Here are the papers, Peter, we're cleared now. Control says we can get off as soon as we like."

" Thanks, Dandy. Ask Major Ellison to get

* Milreis is used here instead of the correct "conto," with which few foreigners are familiar.

her warmed up a little. I'll be over in a tick." He turned to the Brazilian at his elbow.

" I'm exceedingly sorry, but that's impossible; the 'plane cannot carry more than two. If you care to come across you can see for yourself."

They walked across the aerodrome to where the " Thunderbolt's " twin engines were already flinging their challenge to the coppery skies.

" I weigh just on 76 kilos," the would-be passenger protested. " Say twelve stone in your measure. I think I could squeeze into the back there. Look, I'm sure I could."

" With two this 'plane is overloaded," Peter lied glibly. " I'm sorry, but what you suggest is sheer suicide. You haven't forgotten that bang in the middle of the last lap are the Andes? Have you thought of the danger? Besides, you can get a regular 'plane down the coast to Buenos Aires and across from there—Major Ellison will tell you——"

" Squadron-Leader Clintock," the Brazilian laughed, " you evidently don't know who I am. My name is Ramon da Cuyta."

Mentally Clintock whistled. Even across the Atlantic the name of the greatest industrialist and landowner in South America was well known. But outwardly he remained indifferent.

" I'm pleased to meet you, Senhor da Cuyta. I'm very sorry that our first acquaintance is to be marred by a refusal——"

" Half a million," the millionaire cut him

short. "I am serious, Squadron-Leader, deadly serious."

"What's that, Peter?" Paget had just come up in time to catch the figure, but the rest of the sentence, being in Portuguese, was lost to him.

"A million whats?"

"Half a million," Clintock corrected, "half a million milreis. Say six thousand pounds."

"Good heavens, that's steep." Dandy's hand came away from his wallet pocket. Then, with a shrug of his shoulders: "Will he take an I O U? I'll toss you who goes into bankruptcy after we get to New Zealand."

Clintock laughed. "He's offering it, old boy."

"Holy Moses, then it would come in mighty handy. What's it for?"

"To take him to Antofagasta."

Dandy's face dropped. "I knew it. Too good to be true. Come on, let's get into the old crate before he doubles up and we're tempted."

This time the Brazilian misunderstood the only word that meant anything to him.

"Double? Certainly, a million if you wish." Clintock whistled this time out loud.

"Somebody's got sunstroke. O.K., Dandy, up you go. Good-bye, Mr. da Cuyta. No, I'm sorry. Another time perhaps——" The blipping engines sprang to life and drowned the rest of the conversation. Da Cuyta, cramming his hat to his head, his clothes flapping like wild animals, struggled out of the slip stream.

The great grey monoplane gathered speed across the brilliant green, turned skidding, and stood poised, outlined for one second against the tangle of trees and verdure that fringed the flying field. Then the noise of her screws took on an edge; the note lifted as she hurtled forward and slowly cleared the earth. She banked away into a circuit, her under-carriage shrunk and faded into the wings, and then she climbed away into the western sky like the loaded Titan she was.

he electric fuel gauge. Released, the needle
ed and rose a couple of divisions.
ver ninety per cent. empty." Dandy
ed. " That certainly makes things
rd, Peter. Shall I get on to somewhere
e wireless? "
hat's the good? We'd better get down
t away, before the daylight goes. If we
t you can wireless; if we don't—it won't
"
took the controls again and sent the
derbolt " turning downwards in a wide
Dandy fished out a pair of glasses and
o survey the shadowy ground.
esn't look too bad," he grinned.
ock nodded. He did not tell Dandy the
that was uppermost in his mind—that even
got down safely it might well be three
l miles to the nearest town, Goyaz or Leo-
, even presupposing you knew the right
n; and the chances of a wandering cattle-
prospector were very slim.
arth twisted up to meet them, and the sun
ind the bank of clouds that now filled the
sky. At a thousand feet Clintock levelled
set the 'plane in a wider circle, while both
xiously scanned the earth beneath.
gonising minutes passed. Each strained
against the gathering darkness, waiting
rst halting cough in the even drone that

CHAPTER TWO

BEYOND RIO

THE HOURS droned away. The jungle on the coast gave way to the rolling savannahs, the fattening ground of the big meat combines, split by the great silver snake of the San Francisco.

" The same river that we crossed just after starting," Peter told Dandy, " and those are the Parana Mountains."

The blue rim of the home of South America's greatest trade route lifted slowly from the horizon. Signs of civilisation dropped away as they climbed across the foothills, and presently the whole range, brown and grey, spread from the northern horizon to the south beneath them.

" They're going to build their Federal capital hereabout," Peter informed his companion as the Parana range flattened again into a vast rolling plateau. " Funny to think what this country will look like then."

" You can go around in your dotage selling guide books; you'd do fine."

Peter chuckled. Only Dandy knew how dear this project had been to his heart for years. To take a part in the opening up of the last of the world's continents. To continue the work of his father, who had died of fever on the very drainage scheme

15

that was to turn Santos from a white man's grave
to a great industrial centre. In the great empty
plains and forests of Brazil, which so few people
realise is bigger than the United States, lies the
wealth of fifty empires; but transport is difficult.
Brazil is unlucky in her southern rivers and mountains, which form barriers, rather than highways,
to the coast, and pin development and three-
quarters of the population into three states. But
now the aeroplane had come to change all that.
Modern as the " Thunderbolt " was in every line
of her, she was a covered wagon of the Southern
Middle West to Peter Clintock.

Dandy brought him out of his reverie.

" Here comes Ellison's weather ! "

Far ahead, where the setting sun was nearing
the horizon, lay a bank of slate-grey cloud.

" Thunder." Peter shrugged his shoulders.
" Doesn't look very high. Take her up to twelve
thousand and we'll run at that."

Dandy nodded and eased back his stick. The
horizon with its menacing cloudbank dropped from
the forward window as though snatched away by
a mystic hand. Dandy frowned:

" That's funny, Peter; she's pulling almighty
well. I fancied she was flying light awhile back
when we were over the mountains."

" Ellison's boys must have tuned her up better
than we did," suggested Clintock, his eye on the
creeping needle of the altimeter.

Dandy shook his head.

" It's more than that."
back still farther, and the e
end windows of the cabin
we're climbing."

" Let me have her." (
an anxious note.

He grasped his own sti
of the great monoplane l
The 'plane rode evenly,
eddy of the approaching

" Nothing funny abou
mented Clintock; then, a
he eased his stick over a
bolt " rudder.

Obediently the 'plane l
and the endless brown v
fell as Clintock converte

" You're perfectly ri
as though she had no lo
gods, man—look at that

Dandy craned back to
in the back seat, could ju
rear of the " Thunderbo
the fuselage, where, on
her huge petrol tanks,
about three inches apar

" Must have been do
said Clintock grimly.
juice leaking—slipstre
Sound the tanks, Dand

Tight-lipped, he wat

W.B.R.

home
flicker

" O
whistl
awkwa
with th

" W
straigh
make
matter

He
" Thur
circle.
began t

" D
Clint
thought
if they
hundre
poldina
directio
hand or

The e
sank be
western
out and
flyers ar

Ten a
his eyes
for the f

would tell them the engines were starved of petrol and the end had come.

"Look, Peter," cried Dandy suddenly, "beyond that outcrop of rock—go over, go over!"

Clintock reversed the bank of the "Thunderbolt," and the outcrop of rocks fell away beneath them to reveal a wide stretch of even green, broken in the middle by a brown smear of dried water-course. Beyond, a farther ridge of boulders edged the valley, which ran, tapering, for a couple of miles or so, to the south.

"Have to chance the wind," said Clintock, banking again to bring the "Thunderbolt" back over the valley at a lower altitude. "What's your guess?"

"Against the storm at this distance," suggested Dandy, mockingly wetting his finger and holding it up. "Down you go, Peter, while there's still a little bit of light."

Clintock edged the "Thunderbolt" over, chose a particularly even-looking piece of green, and gradually closed his throttle.

The drone of the engines lost its power, and the earth came whistling up. The flat green of the valley broke into a series of undulating slopes, but still no serious bumps appeared. Both flyers waited for the sickening drop that would tell them that the "Thunderbolt," gliding with the wind, had stalled.

Suddenly Clintock shouted: "The undercarriage, Dandy, quick!"

Feverishly Paget threw the electric release, and both flyers breathed again, that in their anxiety about the conditions of landing they had not fore-doomed the whole issue by carelessness.

Now the ground was very near; and almost before they knew for certain that yet another danger was past the "Thunderbolt" had touched.

She bounced badly, and Clintock was for one sickening split second in doubt as to whether or not he should pull out again and try another spot, when the 'plane took matters into her own hands and dropped the remaining few feet.

She came to a jolting standstill; the blipping propellers steadied and were still. The absence of the engines' roar was almost tangible for a moment of blessed relief, and then Dandy, wiping his forehead, said:

"Gracious, Peter, you never made a worse landing—or a better!"

Half an hour later Dandy, screwdriver in hand, gazed nonplussed at the radio panel which he had tilted out across his lap.

"It's no good, Peter," he said with a wry grin, "shorted somewhere after that jolting."

He pushed the useless panel back and screwed it home.

"Three hundred miles," he mused, gazing at the empty valley. "Say fifteen days at twenty miles a day—well, I always said I needed to lose weight.''

Clintock laughed.

'' You've forgotten we're sitting in a perfectly serviceable aeroplane. Now that we've plugged those holes, we are good for three hundred miles with a bit of luck. We can get off as soon as it gets light.''

'' In that case,'' said Dandy, '' I propose to go to sleep.''

He wriggled back to obtain the maximum comfort his tiny cockpit allowed him, and was soon snoring peacefully to the accompaniment of thc first rainlash of the storm that barely an hour before had saved him from a forced landing in the dark, meaning almost certain death.

But Peter Clintock sat studying his map by the light of a torch, pausing occasionally to jot figures down in the margin or to glance anxiously through the streaming window to see if the '' Thunderbolt '' was shifting as the wind tore at her.

Three hundred miles in the tanks, perhaps. Three hundred miles to go, perhaps. And, above everything, in which direction?

CHAPTER THREE

" UP WITH YOUR HANDS, GENTLEMEN!"

THE STORM had blown itself out when Dandy
woke. The sun was streaming across a damp
world, red through the mists that the growing
heat was already sucking up. He sat up and
scratched his bullet head.

" What time is it, Peter?"

Clintock, who had already been awake some
time, looked up with a grin from a page of figures.

" That's just exactly what I'm trying to find
out," he said.

Dandy frowned.

" Why? Has the clock stopped? I thought
the darned thing went for eight days."

" So it does, but it's set to Pernambuco time."

Dandy resumed the head scratching, this time
more vigorously, while Clintock went on:

" As far as I can make out, we came about 1,200
miles yesterday—that squares with our average
speed and the known landmarks that we logged—
so I reckon we're here, about two hundred or so
miles south-west of Goyaz."

" I see," Dandy had leaned backwards to
follow his pencil on the map, " just below the 'o'
in Grosso."

" Yes. That makes us about forty miles from

22

the Araguaya, and the Cayapo Mountains ought to be visible about eighty miles to the south-east. That squares with what I remember of the landscape last night.''

'' Um,'' said Dandy thoughtfully. '' I remember a river of sorts, at least it was an elongated jungle by appearances, but it struck me then that it must be a river.''

Clintock nodded.

'' So that puts us about on the meridian of 53° west.''

Dandy screwed his brow in mental calculation.

'' About 18° west of Pernambuco? Say fifteen into eighteen is one and three over; um-um, a fifth of sixty—um, say an hour and twelve minutes back.''

Clintock laughed.

'' Looks all right on paper,'' he said, '' but the airfield time is standardised. I nearly fell for that one. It's taken from the zone time of 45° west. The same zone as Rio. Get me? That brings it down to 8 degrees. Thirty-two minutes behind.''

Dandy leaned back.

'' Marvellous,'' he wondered, '' truly marvellous, and all so as I can have breakfast on time. What good is it to know the time to the tick?''

'' Just this: that at 6 a.m. the sun is due east from us, and it's rather important for us to know whether the compass is still O.K.''

'' Pardon, professor, pardon, I stand corrected.'' Dandy looked round ruefully. '' At least I would if I had the head room. But, anyway, we're too late—it's just on seven."

" Only six by the sun. You forget that January is summer-time hereabouts."

" I give it up." Dandy opened the cabin top. " I'll have a shave while you carry on with the sun worship."

He climbed out, fetched his travelling toilet case, and went down to where the night's rain had turned the watercourse into a fair-sized stream.

There he proceeded stolidly to shave and wash as calmly as though he were in his own bathroom.

Presently he returned, alternately flicking his hands and wiping them with a sodden handkerchief.

" Pity we didn't bring any towels, Peter. How's the airman's friend?"

" Turned airman's traitor," said Clintock quietly. " That bumping must have messed up the bearings. I've swung her twenty times, and she's inconsistent over nearly thirty degrees."

Dandy clicked his tongue against his teeth.

" Too bad," he said lightly. " Have to sue that blinkin' firm when we get back. Got any bright ideas?"

" Well, we can't just stay here. We'll have to set a course by the sun. We've only got about an hour's juice, so we can't go too far out. Only thing is: I was hoping to get a bearing on one or two prominent landmarks to fix more accurately just where we are."

" That's not a bad scheme, anyway," Dandy nodded, then pointed to where, a mile or so down the valley, a crest of rock rose out of the mists. " See that outcrop? By the time we get there the mist'll be cleared, and we'll be able to get a good look round. In the meantime have we got any of that chocolate left? I'm hungry."

For a moment Clintock hesitated. Then he realised that if they were going to fly—which was by far their best chance—they would either be at a town or beyond the need of food by nightfall. A second lucky landing was too much to ask of the gods.

So they ate their remaining chocolate with gusto.

When they had finished, Dandy smoothed out the wrapper and pencilled on it:

" BACK IN TWO HOURS."

" Just in case anyone felt tempted to pinch the old crate," he explained.

Clintock smiled, despite his sober reflections, and then they both set off down the valley towards the chosen crest of rock.

The valley sloped away towards the north, narrowing fairly sharply. As they approached the crest it became obvious that Dandy had picked on the only nearby piece of high land, and that the ascent was going to be stiff going.

" I tell you what, Peter," said the author of

the plan, " I reckon we'll do better to carry on up to the top of the valley and get at the crest from the far side."

So they turned up the valley again. The heat was already beginning to make their flying kit unbearable, and Dandy, perspiring profusely, proposed a rest.

While they sat there Clintock gazed fixedly at the stream, his brows knit.

" What's up with the drainage, Peter?" Dandy queried.

" It's funny," said Peter, " how this land lies. You see the valley is narrowing——"

" I'll say," Dandy agreed, pointing. " I reckon that bend pretty nearly sees the end of it."

" But it can't. Look, the stream is running towards the narrow end, not away from it. There must be some outlet, unless the whole top end is flooded."

Dandy shrugged his shoulders.

" O.K. Let's go and see; it's all the same to me."

Half a mile farther up and round the slight bend that had previously obscured their view they found that the valley sloped away sharply into a narrow rocky defile, turning the stream into a tossing mass of foam. Here they had to tread carefully, for the sides of the canyon came to within a few feet of the stream, leaving only a broken pathway of wet and slippery rocks.

After half-an-hour's scrambling they saw that

the pass was opening out. A hundred yards farther and the rocky walls gave way, leaving them a commanding view of a basin-shaped hollow some four miles in width and about six miles long, lipped on every side by the rocky soil of the plateau. The bottom of the basin was a smooth expanse of grey sand. Only at the edges did rocks and vegetation break the dead-even curves.

" Darn queer shape, eh?" gasped Dandy, breathing hard from the exertion of his recent rock climbing.

Clintock pursed his lips. " I've seen something of the same once before," he said. " It was probably made by the fall of a colossal meteor thousands of years ago. That accounts for the unusual direction of the stream. Well, it's interesting, but we're not on an official survey, so we'd better get on." His voice rose in sudden surprise: " Half a minute, though, half a minute!"

Dandy, who had already started back, turned sharply at the sudden change in Clintock's voice.

" What's up? "

" Do you see what I see? Down there."

" Crikey, yes; it's a sluice."

" It's something man-made, anyway. I wondered where the stream went to. You see, it's diverted there, and it must go by a culvert, because the natural lie of the land is straight down. I bet you this whole hollow was a lake originally. Probably still would be in flood-time if it weren't for that culvert. But it's mighty queer. There's the irrigation—must have cost a few hundred—but where's the yield? There's no farm, no house, no crops—nothing. What the devil's the idea of it?"

For answer Dandy grabbed his arm and pointed away to their left. "Unless I'm much mistaken, Peter, that's a hut up there. See, just beneath the edge there. And, look, I'll swear there's a couple of tree stumps."

Neck and neck they scrambled, half running, half crawling, across the face of the rocks. Finally they pulled up just short of what had obviously been a clump of sizeable trees. Peter examined the stumps.

"Cut down over a year ago, I'd reckon," he guessed. "But why? What in heaven's name 'ud be the good of clearing ground up here, with thousands of acres unplanted down below?"

"Search me," said Dandy. "Come on, let's see if there's anybody at home."

He started off towards the little timber shanty that stood about a couple of hundred yards away, but Clintock held him back.

"Easy, easy! It doesn't do to rush in on people in this part of the world. They're liable to shoot first and ask for introductions after." Cupping his hands, he bawled:

"Ha qualquer alli?"

Only the echoes answered.

They advanced to within twenty yards of the shanty, and Clintock, still insisting on caution, shouted again.

" Might be asleep," he explained.

But nothing stirred.

Together they ran the last few yards to the shanty. Only to be brought to a standstill in amazement.

One side of the shanty stood open, revealing it as a shelter for, of all things, a searchlight!

It stood there, polished and clean, as incongruous in that virgin wilderness as a top hat on a windjammer.

" I'll eat my sainted aunt," was the only comment Dandy could muster.

Clintock raised an eyebrow.

" It should have a canvas cover," he said quietly, " I hope we haven't disturbed the man who was cleaning it."

He had hardly expressed the thought when a high clear voice behind them ordered:

" Up with your hands, gentlemen. If you move an inch I'll shoot."

Instinctively they obeyed. The voice was that of a boy, but it carried a crisp conviction that the owner meant what he said.

Came a clatter of horse's hooves and there rode out from behind a hummock of rock a small man on a wiry grey mare. Slung at the ready across his saddle-bow was a very efficient-looking rifle.

CHAPTER FOUR

AWAITING SENTENCE

" TURN ROUND," the stranger ordered sharply.
" Turn round and follow that pathway down.
But keep your hands up."

From the front of the shanty, with its mysterious contents, a narrow pathway zigzagged into
the hollow, and down this the two aviators picked
their way. Their captor rode about twenty yards
behind, the mare treading daintily down the slope
with the ease of familiarity.

For about two-thirds of the way down the slope
was covered with rough bushes and a sprinkling of
fair-sized shrubs. As they neared the edge of
these Dandy said quietly:

" Let's make a break for it, Peter, before we get
clear of any cover. Lower down it would be
hopeless."

" Not worth it," Clintock replied without
turning his head. " We're cut off from the 'plane
and this fellow can't be alone. Even if we gave this
one the slip, they'd only turn a dozen men out
to look for us. Better go on and see what happens;
they'll probably be quite friendly if they think
we can do them no harm."

They reached the bottom of the slope, and in
accordance with another curt direction from

behind they turned and followed the edge of the basin towards the culvert that had first aroused their curiosity.

On the level the going was much easier, and there was now the possibility of taking another quick glance at the horseman behind. Dandy was was the first to do so, and caught his breath with surprise.

" Peter, Peter," he whispered out of the corner of his mouth, " it's not a man—it's a girl."

Clintock nodded.

" I was half wondering if it was. But be careful "—for Dandy was beginning to let his arms sag—" being a girl won't make that rifle fire any the worse. I've heard that some of these up-country women are better shots than men."

" Quit talking," sang out the figure on the horse suddenly, closing in on them a little, " and keep looking ahead. If you turn round I'll shoot."

This time there was no doubt about it. It was a woman's voice.

In this fashion they skirted the hollow for nearly a mile. Then Clintock, judging her suspicions to be a little lulled, addressed the girl over his shoulder:

" How did you know we were English? "

For a moment there was silence, then the rider answered:

" I saw the registration letter on your 'plane when you circled over last night. It was kind of you to save me riding right up the valley to get you.''

'' I don't like the sound of that ' Get you,' '' whispered Dandy with a grimace, but out loud he said:

'' You speak pretty good English. Where did you learn? ''

'' Mind your own business,'' the girl replied sharply, and then added, '' And you speak good Portuguese.''

'' Not me,'' said Dandy. '' Peter here is master of a few phrases—but I can't manage more than ' Bons dias.' ''

He had used his usual sarcastic method in referring to Clintock's fluent Portuguese, but to his surprise Clintock took him up.

'' I learned them out of a guide book before I came here.''

Before Dandy could ask for an explanation the conversation, such as it was, was broken up by the appearance of a long, low fazenda built right against the cliff face, and so overgrown with creeper as to be almost invisible at any distance. Behind it the stream splashed out of the culvert in a miniature waterfall, and went gurgling out of sight away round the far side of the hollow.

A heavily-built man, in the traditional dress of the cattle country, was seated on the veranda, in earnest conversation with a slight hatchet-faced fellow of about forty. They both stopped talking as the party approached.

" Hé!" shouted the girl in Portuguese, " I've got them. Juan and Margulies went round the lower way to the 'plane. But I spotted them climbing up the gorge from the top valley. You can drop your arms now." This last to Peter and Dandy in English.

" Thank goodness for that, anyway," said the irrepressible Dandy. " Mine were aching like blazes!"

They stood in the shadow of the fazenda enjoying the relief from the now overpowering heat of the day, while a fierce discussion raged in Portuguesc between the two men and the girl. Eyeing them quietly, Peter said:

" Don't let on that I speak the lingo, Dandy, this is interesting."

He assumed a facial expression of blank indifference.

The discussion seemed to have developed into an argument between the hatchet-faced man and the girl on one side, and the big man on the other.

" Any idea what they're saying," whispered Dandy, after about ten minutes of fierce gesticulation.

" Can't catch all of it," Peter murmered back. " The girl has told them how she caught us. They seemed to be very annoyed because we saw that lamp. The big fellow with the black moustache is called Leopold, and he wants to shoot us here and now. The other's the Administrador. That means he's the boss of this outfit, whatever it is. He wants to wait for instructions from the chief."

" Then they must have a telephone or something."

" I doubt it. More probably the chief's away, but he's expected back. I'd like to know what's in those two out-houses beyond there. They're some size for a small place like this."

" So would I," said Dandy with a sour expression. " It'll be such a comfort when we face the firing squad. Aha, here comes the casting vote."

Round the out-houses which had attracted Peter's attention rode about a dozen men. Unkempt, mostly unshaven, and their clothes little above rags, they presented a picture to make a film producer green with envy Every man was armed to the teeth.

Two of the new arrivals, evidently the leaders, dismounted and strode up to the veranda.

" Let's hope they're nice, kind men at heart," said Dandy airily, " otherwise that swings the voting in favour of our immediate disposal."

After an exchange of questions and answers two more men were called from the group. The man who was called Leopold rapped out an order and the two horsemen drew their revolvers and advanced on the flyers.

" Stand steady," said Peter quietly, " they're only going to lock us up."

And so it proved to be. With many gestures and much brandishing of revolvers the two horsemen, both of whom appeared to be of Indian stock, ushered Clintock and Paget past the two out-houses to where, still against the cliff-face and even more obscured by creepers than the fazenda, stood a fairsized bunk-house, evidently the men's sleeping quarters. The far end of this had been partitioned off at some time to make a sort of store-room, though it was now empty. But the contents had once justified a huge lock and bar on the solid quebracho door.

Into this the boys were shoved. The door slammed to behind them, and they heard the lock turn and the bar drop into place.

For a few seconds they stood in the half darkness, then Clintock put his eye to a crevice in the boarding, and watched their two guards, apparently well satisfied, settle down against the bunkhouse wall and light a long Brazilian cheroot between them, passing it silently one to the other in the Indian fashion.

" Well," said Dandy on receipt of this piece of information, " what next?"

" I don't quite know," said Clintock thoughtfully, " but one thing intrigues me."

" What's that?"

" The last thing that friend Leopold said before they took us away was: ' It would be fatal if they saw anything to-night. I say shoot them and burn the aeroplane with the bodies in it.' "

Dandy rubbed his chin thoughtfully. " I bet that fellow smells," he said.

CHAPTER FIVE

A STRANGE DINNER PARTY

WITH THE AID of a box of matches, they explored their prison. The place was strongly built, even to the partition wall that divided them from the rest of the bunk-house. What light and air that came in did so through chinks in the roughly hewn boards. The floor consisted of earth, baked dry and hard as iron.

A pile of old sacks in the corner was the only thing to sit on. In the other corner a butt was lodged in a cross timber and contained a few inches of water and a small iron cup.

" I shouldn't," Clintock cautioned Dandy, who was about to scoop himself up a drink. " It looks clean enough, but it's just as likely to carry typhus as not. Better to leave it until things get really bad—if they keep us in here that long."

They settled down as comfortably as the sacks would allow, and sat for a short time in silence. The heat in the totally enclosed room was terrific; Clintock suggested taking off some clothes, and presently the pair of them were squating semi-naked in the oppressive gloom.

" Harking back to the gent who got us into this mess," Clintock started a conversation, " I don't think it was da Cuyta."

" I don't see who else it could have been,"
argued Dandy.

" I admit he's the natural person to suspect,"
Clintock agreed, " but remember he never went
near the side of the 'plane where the holes were.
And another thing, he'd hardly try to wreck a
'plane he was trying to bag a seat in at a very
generous price."

Dandy wriggled round on the sacks, trying to
find a more comfortable position.

" That's all very well," he said, " but suppose
his dodge was to keep our attention on his side of
the 'plane while some other cove put a couple of
bullets into our tanks."

" There wasn't anybody on the other side,"
Peter objected.

" Not that we remember, but a mechanic
wouldn't have looked a bit out of place. The
engines would cover a small calibre gun with a
silencer, and the bulk of the juice in the tanks
would stop the bullet going clean through. It was
well thought out."

" Huh," Clintock grunted, " I'm full of admiration. But still, even supposing that was how
it was done, what was the big idea?"

" Search me. Anyway we can count our bless-
ings it didn't come off. We don't seem a great
success in Brazil, do we?"

" There's just one thing," Clintock resumed,
after another silence. " It is possible that da Cuyta
plugged us as we were taking off, purely out of

pique. Most Brazilians are like children when their will is crossed—especially the men, because they're nearly always spoiled as youngsters. And every one in South America is handy with a gun. What do you think of that for an idea?"

" Sounds a bit tall," Dandy commented, " but then this is a tall country."

And thus they passed the day alternately talking and dozing. Once or twice Clintock went over to the door and peered out through the space between the hinges. But the two guards still sat there; and when, shortly after midday, they went away, presumably to get some food, two more came and relieved them. The only sound was the chirping of cicadas.

Just about sunset they were both wakened to life by the sound of the bar being removed from the door. It was the hatchet-faced Administrador who came in, followed by the two peons with drawn revolvers.

He looked at the two airmen, who had stood up to greet him, and his features twisted into what, in a kinder face, would have passed for a smile.

" Plenty hot, ha?" he asked in a thick, broken accent.

" Warmish," said Dandy.

Again the parody of a smile crossed the Administrador's face.

" Maybe sometime soon we heara what we gotta make with yous—no? Then maybe we make yous plenty more hots—eh?"

" Look here," said Peter with a show of temper, " we're British subjects, and if you don't let us go we'll make it hot for you when we get in touch with the authorities."

" Autorities," mimicked the hatchet-faced man, " you know soon, I's autorities in here. You get-a the clothes. Come."

" Better do what he says," said Peter. " He doesn't seem to react any too well to threats."

They pulled on their trousers again and followed the Administrador out of the shed. The two peons followed behind, silent as a pair of hounds. Only the threatening revolvers revealed the fact that they took any interest in the proceedings at all. Clintock decided to try another line.

" My father," he lied glibly, " owns a frigori-fico in San Paulo. He has a big fazenda near Barretos. He'd pay a pretty big ransom for us."

" Plenty money—ha?"

" Plenty. Maybe a million milreis each."

There was no point in lying on a small scale.

The man turned to him with a leer.

" I guess he make-a very nice stone for yous. Say ' Thees stone remember my nice son '—eh. Pretty good—no?"

Dandy laughed.

" Wonderful sense of humour," he said to Peter confidentially.

That seemed to conclude the conversation. They followed in silence up the steps of the veranda and into the living-room of the fazenda. A table, lit by an oil lamp slung from the ceiling, was set for five persons. Placed on the table were five incredibly ancient dinner knives, a tin of square, hard biscuits, evidently the local substitute for bread, four tin plates and one of china, and a two-litre bottle of pinga, a sort of cheap spirit made out of cane.

Following a series of suggestions by gesture they seated themselves. Peter on a sugar box, and Dandy on an upturned kerosene drum.

" We appear to have strained the local capacity for entertaining," commented the latter. " Still, I don't care so long as I get something to eat."

A few moments later, Leopold swaggered in from an adjoining room and seated himself opposite. The Administrador took the head of the table, a trestle affair, which in contrast to everything else about the fazenda appeared to have been designed for its present use.

They sat, all four, in silence. The two guards squatted on the steps of the veranda. From somewhere had come a gourd of maté, which they sucked in turn through a metal tube. This vigorous sucking was the only thing audible.

" I like the orchestra," said Dandy, after about a minute's silence. " Are we waiting for the fatted calf, or is somebody going to say grace?"

Leopold stared at him woodenly; the Administrador, engaged in vigorously picking his nose, evidently chose to ignore the remark, if he understood it.

And then the girl came in carrying a great dish-ful of food. For the first time they had a chance to size her up at leisure. She was small, and even the men's clothes that she wore could not mask a certain natural grace of carriage. Her features were petite to a point of fierceness, a suggestion much aided by a mop of flaming red hair, and a pair of alert blue eyes. The general effect was piquant, more than pretty. They noticed that, in contrast to everybody and everything about the place, her clothes were reasonably neat, and her hands clean.

She nodded curtly to the two flyers, plonked the dish in the centre of the table and seated herself.

Without more preamble, Leopold and the Administrador began diving at the pile of food, scooping at it with a knife and a biscuit. The girl waited till they had helped themselves to their satisfaction, and then took a smaller portion in similar fashion, but without splashing any on the table.

" You too." She nodded again to Dandy and Peter.

Nothing loath, they fell to. The food was the first, barring chocolate, they had had in thirty strenuous hours. Peter tipped half the residue into his tin, and Dandy, after a doubtful glance at the other two men took the rest.

The food was a mixture of vegetables and maize, in which occasionally one found strips of xarque, a sort of dried thong of meat that is common throughout South America. The whole concoction was highly flavoured with some hot spice and more than a suspicion of garlic. Lest the ingredients should retain the slightest suggestion of individuality, it seemed, the whole mess had been stewed and the water drained off.

But it was food, and hot. And that was evidently enough for these fazendieros. They only paused occasionally for a gulp of spirit, both the men and the girl drinking from the bottle.

Dandy, again doubtful of the lengths to which they were expected to participate, grasped the neck of the bottle and looked round.

Neither Leopold nor the Administrador lifted their heads from wolfing their food. Gratefully he swallowed a few mouthfuls and passed the bottle to Peter.

The spirit was as raw as petrol, with a kick like a horse, but after those sweltering hours in their improvised jail, the flyers had a thirst past any nice discrimination.

In this manner the five of them disposed of both food and drink at a high speed. The girl and Dandy, who happened to be seated opposite her, were the first to finish. He caught her eye across the table.

" That was good," he ventured.

She nodded, but Dandy was not to be put off by an unpromising beginning.

" What's your name?" he asked.

" Alison," she told him.

Clintock glanced up, surprised.

" You must be Scotch."

" I'm an American."

Something in the tone of her voice made both men look at her sharply. There had come to her words an edge, a suggestion of fierce conviction that loaded the simple statement with a meaning that the sense of the words belied. Even Dandy was taken back.

" From the States, eh?" he said, and then added lamely, " I was in New York once."

" You fool," the girl blazed out suddenly. " Have you ever looked at a map? Who told you America stopped at the borders of Mexico?"

She pointed out across the veranda to the darkened hollow.

" There is America. All that is America, a thousand miles east and west. Two thousand north and south is all America. The old America, the first, the richest and the greatest America."

The Administrador looked up and made some curt comment in Portuguese.

Her voice had risen to a cry. Dandy shifted in his seat.

" I'm very sorry," he murmered, " I didn't mean to offend you; it's just a question of names, you see—"

He felt incapable of explaining himself. All the time he was searching his mind for a memory that eluded him. Where had he seen eyes that gazed calmly out of a wild face, where had he heard words with that unusual high-pitched ring, marked by that imperious pointing gesture before?''

And suddenly it came back to him. The scene so familiar to London's Sunday crowds. A long-haired orator, a rough platform, with its crudely-lettered slogan, surrounded by a good-humoured, critical audience.

'' Reminds you of Hyde Park in election time,'' he said quietly to Peter.

But Clintock was not listening. He had heard the Administrador say quietly to Alison:

'' Gently, my child, you are not in Buenos Aires on the Boca now.''

He had never been to the capital of the great Southern Republic, but he had heard enough of the talk of men on ships going backwards and forwards to England as a child to know that the Boca was the great waterfront waste ground, the gathering place of down and outs, criminals and casual dock-hands, the sweepings of the gutters of every nation, living on what they could filch and a ticket in next week's lottery. And what in heaven's name was the connection between that and this lonely fazenda on the edge of the Brazilian matto?

Ignoring Dandy, he said to the girl:

'' You speak English remarkably well. Surely you must have been abroad at some time?''

Alison had calmed down. The fire in her eyes had gone as rapidly as it had come. She said casually:

'' My mother was Scottish. She died when I was

very young. My father died four years ago. I have always worked up here in the cattle lands. I went as far as Goyaz once, where the railway is, but I didn't like it. I learned the English from my mother. Some of the managers up here are English, so I can practise now and then."

" I see," said Clintock. But mentally he noted, " The girl's a magnificient liar!"

CHAPTER SIX

ESCAPE!

THEREAFTER a deadlock followed for some minutes.

Dandy was tempted to pinch himself to break the dream. Only the carrying handle of the kerosene drum, which, no matter how he settled, always stuck into him, kept him conscious of the fact that this was indeed sheer, hard reality. Peter had enough startling material to turn over in his mind to keep him occupied. Leopold and the Administrador did not appear disposed to conversation; Alison seemed bent on studying the reaction of the flyers to her brief autobiography.

Suddenly Leopold, leaning back on his chair, shouted lustily:

" José! Hé, José! Bring the coffee."

A few seconds later there appeared a little wizened man, with the shuffling carriage and shifty eyes of extreme old age, but the face and hands of a child. He carried, using the side of a packing case as a tray, two ancient and battered mugs, an iron drinking bowl, and two tins that in their former glory had left the Middle-west full of a famous brand of pork and beans. Each container was filled to the brim with a steaming black liquid, which the carrier's unsteady hand had slopped, so that the improvised tray swam in coffee, whence it dripped mournfully to the floor.

José paused beside Leopold, who, seizing a mug in each hand, thrust one in front of the Administrador, and took the other himself. Camp manners know little of the city niceties, so it was left to Dandy to help Alison to the drinking bowl, distinctly the best of the three remaining vessels, and to take the two tins for Peter and himself.

His mission accomplished, José stood, tray in hand, staring at the flyers as though they were from another world.

"Get out!"

Leopold addressed him as though he were a dog; and that in a continent where dogs are treated worse than anywhere else on earth.

José's watery brown eyes dilated from interest to panic, and he shuffled back to the kitchen.

"This," said Alison, "is a luxury you wouldn't get in London. It's pure mocha."

"You do yourselves well here," said Dandy, turning his tin in a vain search for an edge that was not jagged.

"We get this right up from the coast," Alison explained.

"And your salt too," said Peter, picking up and examining the small block of the mineral that stood ungarnished on the table. "That must come a long way."

" The Administrador is very generous," Alison told him.

" Crikey," said Dandy, trusting to this latter's paucity of English, " he doesn't look it."

Alison laughed; a little, silvery laugh, gentle and obviously genuine.

" You know," said Dandy, " if you'll forgive me saying so, that's the first really pleasant sound I've heard in this valley."

The girl blushed.

" You'd better drink your coffee," she said pertly.

But the coffee drinking was a slow process, owing to its intense heat. Dandy was heartened to another onslaught.

" I quite begin to like this place," he lied. " How long would you say we shall be here?"

" That all depends; we shall probably get instructions what to do with you to-night."

" Instructions? From whom?"

The girl shook her head.

" Never mind," she said, seeming for the moment uncertain as to whether she had gone too far. " You'll know when we get them."

By the time they had finished the coffee, it was pitch dark, and the moon had risen. It was about full now, and the yellow orb hung low over the eastern lip of the hollow like a lamp, bathing the vast expanse of unbroken sand in a mist of soft light.

Leopold consulted an enormous turnip top

watch, which he produced from the inner recesses of his voluminous clothing. Sucking his teeth, he gazed at the dial, seeming wrapped in mental calculation. Then he leaned over and whispered fiercely to the Administrador.

The latter nodded, putting down a pencil and notebook with which for the past ten minutes he had been engaged, and smiled across at the flyers.

" Come," he said, indicating the door.

The man's face was reminiscent of thin green ice, with a hole in it.

" It appears to be our bed-time," remarked Dandy, getting to his feet. " Good-night, Miss Alison."

The girl, too, had risen and she stood gazing fixedly at him, her mouth moving slightly in an indecisive search for words.

" Good-night," she said at length, extending her hand to him as though on an impulse.

" Why—er, good-night," repeated Dandy as he shooks hands, at a loss for anything else to say.

He turned and followed Clintock out on to the veranda. Ahead walked the Administrador with a lantern, behind the inevitable guards with revolvers drawn.

From the bunk-house came a long-drawn-out, undulating wail, rising and falling like the wind, as numerous voices took it up or dropped out. The peons were evidently in good spirits.

" It passes for singing up here," remarked Clintock.

They turned into the store-room again. The Administrador tilted the lantern so that the flickering light fell on their faces.

" Good-nights," he said with mock politeness. " I teenk you sleeps preety nice in here—no?"

" Very nice, thank you," Dandy assured him.

Followed by the two peons he stalked out. The door slammed; came the familiar noise of lock and bar being turned against them, and the Administrador's footsteps faded into the wailing uproar from the adjoining bunk-house.

Clintock waited for some seconds, eye to the crack in the door, till he was sure the guards had settled down.

" Now," he said incisively, and moved quickly across to the water butt. He scooped up a cupful of lukewarm liquid, produced from his pocket the cake of salt he had been examining at table, and scrunched a chunk of salt into the water.

" What's the big idea?" asked Dandy, amazed.

" You're going to be sick."

" But I don't want to be sick."

" Never mind about that. That coffee, man, did you ever taste anything so sour before? Pure mocha my foot!"

" Mine was too hot to taste," said Dandy, " but look here, Peter——

" Don't argue,' Clintock thrust the cup of brine into his unwilling hands, and then as Dandy still seemed uncertain, " Go on. Over in that corner and drink it before the dope gets a hold on you."

" Dope?"

" Yes. In the coffee, you half-wit. Give you a pretty girl to look at and anybody could pinch your soul. That's the spirit," he added, as the brine took violent effect.

" But she is pretty, isn't she?" said Dandy between his spasms, " oough!"

" Very," said Peter. " Make room."

He, too, had dosed himself with the vile-smelling brine.

And between them they made a good job of it. Clintock, ever cautious, insisted on a second dose.

" Now what about a drink of ordinary water?" asked Dandy when it was all over.

Clintock shook his head.

" No sense in taking unnecessary chances."

" But if it's infected we've already taken it."

" Yes, but not for long. Cover up the evidence with one of those sacks."

" O.K." Dandy obeyed ruefully. " Poor little germs. I should feel most thwarted if I were treated like that."

" I dare say," Peter laughed. " Sit down here, and the moment you feel drowsy, say so."

" I do now."

" I thought so, staring up at a lovely pair of eyes, and lapping up dope like honey. Oh, no, you don't!"

He caught Dandy and prevented him from sitting down. " Quietly, now. Quiet."

He himself felt the first waves of the drug cloying at his brain. The singing in the bunk-house became distorted, swelling to ear-splitting volume, and then receding to a great distance.

Grinding his teeth, he set himself to pace up and down their prison, dragging Dandy, protesting like any drunkard, with him. For ten minutes he kept up this staggering pantomime, then fortune deserted him.

He tripped on the uneven floor, and the pair of them collapsed in a heap. From a great distance Dandy heard Peter's voice, appealing like a man in mortal pain.

" Dandy. Get up. We've only got to fight this off and we can get back to the 'plane. Only got to fight, only got—only got to——"

The voice tailed off into senseless repetition. Slowly Dandy knelt up, each movement a wilderness of laborious unco-ordinated effort. He flung back his head as though defying a multitude of challenging foes. With a supreme effort he struggled to his feet and stood, arms outstretched, fighting for his balance.

He gave Peter a vicious kick.

" Clintock," he abjured solemnly, " get up. You're behaving like a fool! Get up!"

The remark was pointed by another heavier kick.

Clintock stirred. Bending over him, Dandy

picked an arm out of the darkness and hoisted him viciously up. This time fortune smiled; the shapeless pillar of swaying humanity stayed erect.

" Now," said Dandy fiercely, " now, we gotta get back. Gotta get back; see. Before they closh the gates!"

And he set about pacing the prison with even more determined vigour than Clintock had done.

Their breath rasping between clenched teeth, sweat pouring off them, they kept up the staggering battle against the fumes of the drug for another quarter of an hour. Gradually the exercise had effect. The good physical condition of both of them told immensely in their favour, coupled with the rapid removal of the doped coffee.

About an hour after they had returned to their prison, Clintock was satisfied that they had both ridded themselves of the narcotic sufficiently to tackle the next stage of his plan.

" How do you feel?" he asked Dandy.

" Terrible," was the answer. " The worst ever. My head aches like blazes, and my stomach feels as though a horse had kicked me."

" After the trick, sugar," laughed Peter, and he produced from his pocket half a dozen of the dry biscuits that had been on the supper table. Three of these he handed to Dandy.

" Eat 'em slowly," he advised. " Remember the only food you've eaten for a dickens of a long time isn't with you any more."

Dandy's grimace by way of reply was lost to

him in the darkness. Together they sat and munched the bone dry biscuits. Dandy thinking longingly of the forbidden water in the corner. He was about to make another appeal to Peter to relent and let him have a drink, when their attention was focused on the bunk-house by the abrupt cessation of the concert, which had till then continued with unabated monotony.

They heard a couple of curt orders and the sound of the men moving out to where the horses were tethered. Came shouts and brief instructions, and the party split up, riding away in small sections, each in different directions. The silence was broken by the sound of footsteps coming round to their end of the bunk-house.

" Quick," ordered Peter, " get down and pretend that the coffee had effect."

A moment later the door opened and Leopold strode in swinging a torch from side to side. Clintock and Paget lay supine, the former propped limply against the far wall, while Dandy stretched full length on the floor, shaking the universe with a series of long wavelength snores.

Leopold nodded, satisfied. He strode across and waved the torch under Clintock's face. Peter retained the expressiveness of a waterlogged pudding. Turning, the big fazendiero lumbered back to Dandy and lifted him over with his foot. Dandy responded with an ear-splitting snore. His suspicions completely lulled, Leopold grunted to the two peons who had come up to the open door, and stalked out. Once again the door was locked and barred. The footsteps died away, the snores from the store-room decreasing with them.

" Easy, easy," whispered Peter, for now that the rumpus next door was gone the noise of every movement seemed magnified. " Go quietly to the door and see if he's taken the guards."

Dandy surveyed the moon-lit vista from the crack, slewing his head round to command a view in both directions.

" Yes," he whispered back, " there's nobody there."

" Better wait a bit," counselled the ever-cautious Peter.

They sat for ten long minutes, listening. Nothing stirred outside the store-room. Even the insects had quietened. It seemed as though the whole hollow were waiting for something.

At length Clintock got up and went fumbling in the corner where the water butt was.

" Are you having a drink, you old fool?" asked Dandy, suspicious lest Clintock should have given in at last.

" No," said Clintock with a chuckle, as he went across to the door, " I'm getting the tool bag."

" Tool bag?"

Dandy moved over to his side and found him vigorously plying a light but fair-sized screw-driver.

" Where on earth did you get that from?"

" You brought it."

" I did?"

" Yes. It's the one you used on the wireless cabinet last night. It's been sticking in the leg pocket of your overalls all day. You must have slept with it there."

" I remember it this morning now you mention it," Dandy said. " It got in the way when we were walking up the valley. I had half a mind to chuck it away, but it's the only one we've got."

" Um," was Clintock's comment. " You dropped it all right when you stripped to cool off at midday. I put it up there in case Leopold or any of his friends spotted it.

" Why didn't you tell me?"

Clintock gave him an old-fashioned look.

" You might have mentioned it in the course of your dinner-table chit-chat," he said dryly.

Clintock had studied the big iron lock by daylight, and spotted that the whole thing could be unscrewed from inside the store-room. The lock, like most, was designed to keep people out, not in.

After a few minutes wrestling, the plate on the back of the lock was off. Feeling with his fingers, Clintock engaged the screwdriver on the holding bar and gently prised it back into an unlocked position.

" Stage one," he said to Danby triumphantly. " Now get as many of those sacks as you can and shove them under the door, one on top of the other."

The door had an inch or more clearance over the

ground, and by dint of many manœuvres and skinning his fingers, Dandy contrived to rig a mat of three thickness of sacks just outside. Off the last sack Clintock tore a piece some three feet long, and about two inches wide. This he poked through the crack in the door above the wooden bar that still held them in, dangling it down so that, with the aid of the screwdriver he could retrieve its lower end below the bar.

" Got it," he breathed. " Now for the big chance."

Gently, inch by inch, he lifted the bar in the loop of the sacking. The sockets outside were well worn and the bar lifted loosely.

" Now," said Clintock, when he judged he had raised the looped-up bar well above the nearest socket, " this is where you do the strong man act, Dandy. Get the screwdriver through the crack and press down with all your might."

In this fashion Dandy was able slowly to pivot the heavy bar on the loop of sacking which Clintock held firm from above him. Gradually he forced the short end of it down so that the far end came up out of the socket they could not get at.

After three unsucessful attempts the far end of the bar came clear. Dandy gingerly drew back the screwdriver a little, not daring to relax the pressure, and then gave an outward shove. At the same moment Clintock released his hold on the loop of sacking, and the bar thudded on to the mat of sacks which they had placed to break the sound of its fall.

"Quick," ordered Clintock as he swung the door open, "chuck those sacks inside and put the bar back in place. Now up the back here."

They squeezed along between the bunk-house and the cliff that here bounded the hollow like a wall, pausing only at the open space between the bunk-house and the nearest of the two big sheds that separated the bunk-house from the fazenda itself.

"Got to chance it," said Peter. "We know no other way out. Come on."

He stepped quietly out into the moonlight and started cautiously across the forty yards of open space. Dandy followed close behind.

They had made about half the distance when Clintock suddenly froze, forcing Dandy into immobility with an iron-hard grip on his arm.

Across the hollow from the far lip, splitting the moonlight as though it were inky darkness, swung the violet tinged, all-revealing beam of a powerful searchlight.

CHAPTER SEVEN

BOMBS!

" DOWN," rapped out Clintock. " Down on your face and don't move a muscle."

They flung themselves flat on the hard earth. For seconds that seemed like hours, the beam swung slowly and relentlessly towards them. Then the night became alive with a seering flood of white light, blotting out the rest of the world, and passing as suddenly as it had come.

" They've missed us!" Dandy was upon his knees in an instant; but Peter pulled him down again.

" Stay still, you fool. He'll probably swing back before we can get to cover."

Surely enough the light came to the end of its arc barely a hundred yards behind them, and Dandy scarcely had time to get down again before the beam was on them. But again it passed on without hesitation.

" Now," said Clintock, " run for it."

But Dandy hesitated.

" You go, Peter," he said wildly, " I'm blind. I can't see."

" Come on." Clintock, who had carefully shaded his own eyes in the crook of his arm, took him by the hand. " Run for it. It's perfectly level."

Together they doubled across the rest of the space, and a few seconds later they were panting in the shelter of the nearest shed.

Hardly had they got to cover than the beam swung over the ground again, to be joined by two more, then another and yet another until eight lights in all were sweeping across the hollow, flooding it with light, and turning the night into day.

" Listen," said Dandy suddenly. " Do you hear it?"

Through the stillness of the night came a faint drone, growing gradually louder. First the sound approached from the east, then passed to the north of the hollow. For a few seconds they lost it, then suddenly they picked it up again, now much stronger and passing overhead.

" Making a circuit of the place," commented Dandy, " What do you reckon she is?"

" Either a flight of three or a multi-engined 'plane; pretty heavy engines too. Doesn't carry any navigation lights apparently."

Dandy nodded. His eyes were becoming accustomed to the moonlight again, and he peered cautiously over Clintock's shoulder.

" Well, they'll never get him mucking around like that," he opined.

As though in answer to his criticism all the lights save three suddenly dowsed. Those remaining held steady, focused on a point out of sight on the far side of the hollow.

" I don't get this." Dandy scratched his head.

" I do," said Clintock. " He's going to land. Don't you see they're showing him where the wind is?"

For the huge arrow of light formed by the three beams pointed dead up wind.

" This is evidently well organised," went on Peter. " Listen!"

For about a minute nothing happened. The drone of engines came lower, but continued steadily round the hollow away to the south again. Then the engines cut out, only to pick up again a second later. This performance was repeated several times.

" See," whispered Peter, exultant. " It's a single 'plane and he's blipping his engines to tell them he's got there O.K. and he's coming in. Easy," his voice changed to warning as the other beams were exposed again, " keep your head back."

The 'plane had faded away in the direction opposite to the arrow of light, which now broke up, and joined its fellows to illuminate a great circle near the centre of the hollow.

" My hat!" said Dandy as a thought struck him. " That's why they cut down those trees on the edge of the hollow and diverted the stream. Why, it sticks out a mile. This place would make a marvellous aerodrome."

" Yes," said Peter thoughtfully, " and a very nice one for doing your business quietly. Those lights are being carefully kept below the level of the hollow—see. They'd make the place stand out for miles from the air : As good as an air beacon. But they'd hardly be visible from ground level except for a bit of a glow, and then only from the other side, where the cliff isn't so high. I don't suppose the few people there are around here move by night; the chances of it being spotted are practically nil.''

'' What d'you think is the idea behind it then,'' queried Dandy. '' Smuggling?''

Peter, despite his caution, laughed outright.

'' When will you drop your European standard of geography and realise the size of this country,'' he asked. '' Think for a minute. What in heaven's name 'ud be the good of smuggling anything up here, hundreds and hundreds of miles from the best place to sell it, and next to no means of getting it there. Besides, there's millions of better places for smuggling on the coast, and up the Amazon. No, it's not that. Look. Here she comes. Now perhaps we'll learn something.''

Into the circle of light came gliding a big tri-engined monoplane. The two lights that were to the front of her, immediately dowsed to avoid blinding the pilot; the remainder followed her as she landed perfectly on the smooth hard sands. She passed out of sight, but they heard her taxi round and come to a stop, they judged, in front of the fazenda. As soon as the 'plane was safely settled to a standstill the lights dowsed, and night regained her kingdom that had been so rudely invaded.

Neither of the two Englishmen spoke until the engines of the 'plane cut out. Then Dandy said:

" Say what you like, that was nicely drilled." And then as Peter Clintock did not answer he asked:

" What's eating you now?"

His companion was staring out across the moon-lit hollow, wrapped in thought.

" Her colours," said Peter slowly. " Did you see her colours?"

" Crikey, yes!" Dandy followed the inference. " There was a green, white and blue cockade on the fuselage."

" Green, yellow and blue," corrected Peter, " though I couldn't see the yellow myself. That was due to the lights."

" Then how d'you know it was yellow?"

" Because green, yellow and blue happens to be the colours of the Brazilian Air Force."

Dandy whistled sharply between his teeth.

" The Air Force, eh? Then this must be a government station. That accounts for their taking so much care of us. They think we're spies."

But Clintock was not satisfied with the explanation.

" A government station, without a single flag, not one official inscription, and not a smell of a uniform! Not on your life!"

" Perhaps it's a secret station?"

Clintock shook his head.

" I know they get up to that sort of stunt in Europe," he said, " but not in South America. You couldn't do it. It's flat against the national psychology. Besides if this is a government station somebody round here must be an officer. I grant you Brazilians have their faults, but the educated ones have one never failing virtue: their manners are perfect, especially in the fighting forces. South America is the last stronghold of romantic chivalry. I give you the choice of the Administrador or Leopold for romantic chivalry. No, Dandy, this is no government aerodrome."

" Then what in the name of goodness is it?"

Peter patted his shoulder gently.

" That, little man, is what we may find out if we're good."

He peered out again from behind the shed, only to draw back sharply.

" What is it?" whispered Dandy.

" A whole crowd of them. Coming straight this way."

" Do you think they've spotted us?"

" I doubt it, else they'd be running and shouting. Don't stick your head round like that, you loon. Do it this way."

He got flat on the ground and cautiously advanced his head round the corner. " Any sharp-eyed man might spot you peeping at his eye level, but no sober individual expects a head to come round the corner of a building close to the ground."

" I wasn't in the Boy Scouts," whispered Dandy ruefully, and followed Clintock's example.

Across the hollow from the direction of the recently-landed 'plane was coming a group of men wheeling a heavily-laden trolley. They came on round the shed and started down the long side of the building at the end of which the flyers were hidden.

" Hold it," whispered Peter. " It's no use bunking; they'd hear us for sure. Get back; this is going to be uncommonly close."

They wriggled back out of sight and waited, staring each at the other. The footsteps came on, till their hair bristled with the tension. Dandy wiped the beads of sweat off his forehead with the back of his hand, only to stay, poised rigid, as the footsteps came to a halt a bare twenty feet away.

They heard the quiet issue of orders, the strain and creak of moving metal and wood, and the trolley started forward again. Clintock clenched his fists and gritted his teeth, for only bare seconds stood between them and discovery if the trolley were moving their way.

But the sounds of the wheels and the shuffling were suddenly muffled and died away. Followed silence.

Overcome with curiosity, Dandy, ignoring Peter's forbidding gesture, took a peep round the shed.

About twenty feet away a big trapdoor had opened out of what appeared to be solid earth.

Evidently it gave on to a ramp running below the shed, and down this the trolley had gone.

One man had been left on guard beside the trap-door. Even as Dandy peered round the corner the man turned to glance over his shoulder. At that close distance Dandy recognised the face of José, the misshapen little man who had served the coffee. With a sickening feeling inside his stomach, he realised that the half-wit had seen him, too.

He drew back sharply, and waited for the cry with which José would call the others, but none came. Fortunately for Dandy, those watery brown eyes of José's had sometimes before seen things that were not there, especially on moon-light nights. The little fellow paused, his eyes going from side to side in an agony of indecision. If he called the others and there was no one behind the shed they would laugh at him and kick him because he was afraid of the dark. One could make sure, first; after all, the others were near and one could always shout for help.

He shuffled off towards the corner behind which the flyers hid.

At a sign from Clintock, Dandy stood at the ready, and almost before little José was round the corner a mighty hand closed over his mouth, while an arm seized him from behind in a vice-like hold.

Clintock thrust the knob of the screwdriver which he still carried into his ribs; Dandy caught the lantern and saved it from clattering to the ground.

"Make a sound or move and inch," hissed Clintock in Portuguese, "and I shoot."

Even had he spoken in English, little José would have understood that hard jab at his back. He dropped his arms, his eyes signalling mute submission.

"Quick, Dandy," ordered Clintock. "Nip out and leave the lantern by the trapdoor."

Dandy obeyed. Hardly had he got back to cover when the first of the trolley party scrambled back through the trapdoor. The rest came close on his heels.

"Hé," said a voice, which they recognised as the man Alison had called Margulies, "where's José?"

Peter nodded down on the half-wit by way of translation for Dandy's benefit, jabbing, meanwhile, the screwdriver even harder into the prisoner's back.

"Gone back, I dare say," said another. "He was always afraid of the dark, even moonlight, ever since those vampire bats got him when he was a kid."

"He's left the lantern, anyway," said Margulies. "Shut the trap and stamp down the earth. Come on, let's get in. I'm tired."

There was a general chorus of assent. Present or missing, nobody cared a tinker's cuss about José, anyway.

When the party of peons had gone, Clintock signalled to Dandy to release his grip on the little fellow's mouth, repeating even more villainously, that one shout would spell instant death.

" Hold the gun," he said to Dandy in Portuguese so that José should understand, " and fill him with lead if he calls for help."

José shook his head vigorously to indicate that nothing was further from his mind.

" Now," said Clintock as soon as Paget was in position with the screwdriver, " whisper your answers, and if you tell the truth you won't get hurt. Whose is that 'plane?"

" It is the General's." The wizened little man could hardly gather breath for fright.

" Who is the General?"

" I don't know. I swear by the Holy Mother I don't know. I never saw him."

" Does he come with the 'plane?"

" Sometimes. They said not to-night."

" How often does the 'plane come?" asked Clintock.

Then as the half-wit blinked uncomprehendingly, he put the question into the camp calendar, where the only division of time is the big feasts.

" How many times since last Christmas?"

" Twice," whispered José.

" Always the same 'plane?"

" No. Sometimes smaller."

" Where does he come from?"

José pointed vaguely eastwards.

" Does he go back again."

" No." The pointing finger slewed round to indicate the west.

" Then sometimes he comes from there——" —Clintock pointed from west to east—" and goes that way?"

The half-wit shook his head.

" He goes back a different way. They say he goes back a different way. Never this way."

" Um," said Clintock, " and what does he bring here? What was on the trolley they took down there?"

" I don't know."

" Don't lie," said Clintock sternly, " or I'll tell my friend to shoot you. What was on that trolley?"

Great tears of mortification rolled down José's face, and he raised his little hands in supplication.

" Please, senhor, I do not know. I cannot understand all these things. When I ask they won't tell me. I swear by all the angels it is the truth. Please, senhor, ask your friend not to shoot me. I am very little, and I cannot do you any harm. I do not care to die."

Clintock bit his lip in pity; bullying was not in his line.

" All right," he said gently, " if you can't tell us, you can show us. Do what I say and you won't get hurt."

Sounds from the bunk-house suggested that the

interrupted party had been resumed with gusto; elsewhere all was silent and deserted.

" Come on," said Peter to Dandy, " we'll chance it. I want to have a look down there. Are you game?"

" You bet your life!" Dandy agreed. " Come on, my pretty."

He urged José forward at the point of the screw-driver. They made their way to where the stamped-down earth indicated the trapdoor, Clintock giving Dandy a brief résumé of his questioning on the way.

" Now," ordered Clintock, " show us how it opens."

" They will kill me if I show you." José was trembling from head to foot.

" They won't know," urged Clintock, " and we will certainly kill you if you don't show us at once."

After a second's indecision, José evidently decided that the immediate danger was greater than the future danger. He went over to the wall of the shed and showed them a small lever.

" It goes like this," he said, pulling the lever. " I cannot tell you why. You lean your weight on it and it shuts."

Obediently the great sheet of planking rose from the earth, followed by a quiet thump.

" Counter-weights," said Clintock to Dandy. " Hold him as we go down, in case he tries to bunk in the dark."

But José didn't want to go down.

" It is forbidden," he grovelled piteously.

" Get on." Dandy gave him a jab of the screwdriver which settled the matter.

" He's going to be a nuisance from now on," said Dandy as soon as they reached the bottom of the slope. " You can just see here, but farther in it's pitch dark. Pity we've nothing to tie him up with."

" I know," Clintock agreed, coming up behind. " Let's have the weapon. He addressed the cowering José :

" Stand still." He switched off into English. " I hate to do this, but I'm afraid it can't be helped."

He brought the heavy end of the screwdriver down sharply on the half-wit's head. José collapsed like a sack. Clintock bent down and listened.

" Good," he said, " he's still breathing. I didn't want to kill the poor little chap. That'll keep him quiet for a couple of hours, and, with any luck, we'll be gone by then. I wish now we'd kept that lantern. What do you make of this place?"

" There are racks down this side." Dandy had gone feeling across the dark. " Seems like a wine cellar."

" Um," said Peter. " They take darned good care of their wine. Where are you?"

For Dandy had not moved or answered.

" I'm here," said Dandy, and his voice had grown ten years older. " But they're not wine bottles in the racks"

" What then?"

" Bombs!" said Dandy.

CHAPTER EIGHT

THE ALARM

PETER CROSSED to Dandy's side as quickly as the darkness would allow.

" Here," said the latter, " feel down here."

Lowering his hands, Clintock struck the rough woodwork of a heavily-made rack and, feeling along the shelf, came to the tail fins of what Dandy, who was an armament specialist, had instantly recognised as a bomb.

" What do you make of 'em?"

" Nasty little beggars," said Dandy. " H.E., I should think, and about twenty pounds." His voice became more distant as he felt his way down the rack. " They wouldn't be much good for ordinary military work—not on fortifications worthy of the name—but they'd be just right for intimidation bombing. And—crickey! There's dozens of them. Smaller down here, too. I wouldn't be surprised—yes, darn it! they're incendiaries. Why, this place is a miniature arsenal!"

" It must be," said Clintock thoughtfully. " Remember the General's 'plane had called twice since Christmas. Twice in a month, man! And judging by the way they shoved that trolley, she was well loaded. You're right, Dandy, it's smuggling we've seen to-night. But rather a rare

73

sort of contraband. Now we'd better get out of here."

" O.K.," said Dandy regretfully. " If I'd had a light I could probably have told you where those bombs were made. Now we'll never know."

" Won't we?" said Clintock with a sudden determination. " Listen, Dandy. I vote we try and get to the bottom of this. Are you on?"

" Sure."

" Remember what little José said. If they'd kill him for going down there, shooting 'ud be too good for us."

" I once had my fortune told," said Dandy with mock solemnity. " They said I'd live a long time and have a quiet life, so I joined the Air Force in case they were right. What's the first order, General?"

Clintock laughed.

" The first order is to take life seriously."

" Then the ranks are in a state of mutiny. Come on. Let's get out of here."

They made their way back to the trapdoor. Here the problem of José presented itself.

" Leave him here," Peter decided. " When they find him they'll probably think he fell down and cracked his nut. Or if he comes to, it will keep him quiet for a while, because he'll be too frightened to call for help, as he's in a forbidden place."

So they left litle José where he lay and scrambled up the slope. Dandy pulled on the trapdoor, at first gently, then with all his might, but it stayed firm as a rock.

" Try it with the lever the other way," suggested Peter, going over to the wall and suiting his action to his words.

This time the trap tilted down easily and went home with a slight click. On top of the planks was six inches of earth dried hard like concrete, despite the recent heavy rain. It was only the work of an instant to kick loose earth into the cracks and stamp it down.

" Another day's sun," remarked Clintock, " and you wouldn't know that the earth had been shifted."

Together they crept along behind the two big sheds.

" Don't suppose there's anything much in them," said Clintock in answer to a question from Dandy. " They're probably chiefly meant as a cover to what's underneath. They may use one of them as a hangar, if the 'plane stays over till daylight. Besides, they'd have to give this place some sort of appearance of a normal fazenda."

He paused, for they had reached the end of the second shed. They could now see that the 'plane had taxied up to within fifty feet of the fazenda itself. By her fuselage were a couple of peons; another was under the wings.

Straining their ears, they caught the faint swish swish of a brush being lavishly applied.

" Get it? " whispered Dandy. " They're

painting out her colours and identification marks. Apparently when the General goes west of here he goes in disguise.''

Foot by foot they edged across the open space between the second shed and the fazenda itself. It was nerve-racking going, for had one of the peons happened to glance their way they could not have hoped to avoid detection in the bright moonlight. But the peons were attending to their work with admirable application.

'' Evidently she's going off again soon,'' whispered Dandy when they were safely in the shadow once more. '' Those boys are working in a hurry.''

Clintock nodded and pointed ahead.

From the far end of the fazenda a light was showing. Tip-toeing up, they discovered a window, consisting of a rectangular hole in the wall, which at this point was made of little more than dried mud. The '' window '' was covered with a piece of sacking, through which the light of an oil-lamp filtered. From inside came the babel of fierce argument.

'' They don't use the current for the search-lights to light the place,'' whispered Dandy, his lips to Peter's ear.

The latter shrugged his shoulders.

'' Look out of the picture,'' he replied in similar fashion. '' Listen!''

Dandy obeyed, though the voices from within conveyed nothing to him.

But Clintock soon sorted out the harsh tones of the Administrador and two other men whose voices were unfamiliar. If Leopold was there he was keeping silent.

Gingerly he applied his eye to a chink in the sacking. From this position the Administrador was out of sight to his left, but in his circle of vision came a uniformed young man of about eighteen years and a tall thin fellow of about fifty, with piercing grey eyes and a jaw like a clamp. The younger man had the round face, jet-black hair and deep brown eyes of a Brazilian; the other might have been from any of half a dozen European countries or from the United States, which is very often the same thing. He had an assured carriage which suggested irresistibly to Clintock an aristocratic lineage. The young man in uniform was evidently the centre of the argument.

" That's all very well," he was protesting. " You say everything is ready, but how do I know; what assurance have you to offer me? I come up here and find nothing but half a dozen men and a few miserable huts."

" I'm sorry our hospitality is so poor, Senhor Lieutenant." The Administrador's voice was conciliatory. " But here we have to preserve the appearance of a struggling up-country fazenda, else people might ask questions. At Ithi Caru you will find things different."

" So you say," said the officer, doubting.

" Don't be a young fool, Gomez," the tall man

joined in the persuasion. "Think what you found here. The lights, for instance; does that savour of bad organisation?"

"And you'll find if you go out now that your 'plane is masked and refuelled," added the Administrator.

"How much fuel?" said Gomez petulantly.

"More than enough. We have plenty here, the General sees to that."

"Anyway," the tall thin man clinched the argument, "you can't go back on the thing now you've started."

"Can't I?" flashed Gomez. "Suppose I took the 'plane and flew back. I could tell them where this place is, and——"

"And you'd be the first man to face the firing squad," the Administrador cut him short. "No, my young friend, you're in this up to your neck. Officially, you're dead. Try to come back to life, and you'll be literally dead within a week."

The officer stood nonplussed.

"You promised to tell my mother," he protested.

"That, Gomez, we cannot do," the tall man told him. "Unfortunately, we've had to speed up our plans. People back east are growing a little suspicious, and even the most harmless remark might do untold damage to our scheme. You wouldn't like us to have to threaten her; we could scarcely bring ourselves to do her any harm, but if that were the cruel necessity—no, my friend, you cannot ask me to place her in such danger."

" Have you forgotten the promise you swore to the Senhorita Alison?" asked the Administrador quietly. " She will be very disappointed if you don't keep it. Of course, we could explain that you were worried about your mother, but she might take another view "—his voice dropped to an oily suavity—" she might think you were afraid."

" I'm not afraid," protested the young officer heatedly, " you know that."

" Of course, we do," the tall thin man patted him on the shoulder. " We wouldn't have chosen a coward for this job, Gomez. We don't mind your asking questions. That simply proves that we were right when we picked on you. I admit I doubted myself, but the Senhorita Alison insisted you were the right man; she has a great admiration for you. Think how proud she'll be when she knows that I was wrong and she was right."

" So," thought Clintock to himself, " Alison's the decoy. Dandy'll die of laughing when I tell him that."

" Now," the Administrador was saying, " let's get into the other room and we'll have some food. The regular cook's gone off somewhere, but Leopold is doing his best for you."

The party broke up. The Administrador opened the door for the young lieutenant, and as he passed through the fazendiero raised his eyebrows to the tall thin man who came behind. The later shrugged his shoulders. Nothing passed between them, but Clintock caught a little gesture of the tall man's hand to his side pocket, suggestive of levelling a gun. Evidently it would go hard with Gomez if his loyalty were in any serious doubt.

Clintock was about to step back and tell Dandy what he had heard, when his attention was caught by the sound of running feet at the front of the fazenda.

A peon crashed across the veranda and through the far room, almost colliding with the party in the doorway.

" What is it?" snapped out the Administrador.

" The English," gasped the peon. " They have escaped. " They have been in the cellar. Pedro and I went to oil the generator, and we found José at the bottom of the slope unconscious. We went back to the storehouse, but they are not there."

For a second there was silence. Then the Administrador shouted:

" Rouse every one. If they have been in the cellar they must not escape alive. Get the horses and surround the valley. They can't have got far. Wait! Tell Margulies to send two men up to their aeroplane at once. And four more up to the top lights, so that we can sweep the whole place. Tell every one to shoot them on sight. And shoot to kill!"

CHAPTER NINE

" So what?" was Dandy's comment as Peter translated the shouting to him.

" Nothing for the minute. Hang on and see which way things are going."

They listened. The shouting from the front of the fazenda went down towards the distant shed, there to be joined by a hubbub from the bunkhouse. They gauged that the whole crowd was standing at the entrance to the cellar demanding information from the unconscious form of José. Presently they heard Leopold shouting for a bucket of water; evidently more kindly methods of reviving José had failed.

Inside the fazenda itself all was quiet.

" The last place you look for a mouse is in the cat's basket," said Clintock as he swung a leg through the window. " Come on, Dandy."

The room was fair-sized and, in comparison to the rest of the fazenda, well furnished. It contained three chairs, all of a cheap unpolished wood, and an ancient roll-topped desk. On the wall behind the desk hung a map of South America, marked here and there with little red circles. Peter crossed over and studied it.

" So we're at Lower Valley," he said. " I've

wondered what they called this place." He studied
the position of the other circles. Three were in
the eastern states of Brazil; three more trailed
north-westwards from the borders of Brazil to
Bolivia; one lay to the south, he judged in Paraguay, for the borders of the smaller states were
not indicated, only the towns and physical
features. The Argentine had only one circle, up
in the foothills of the Andes. These circles were
reinforced by a multitude of blue dots, in which
every republic shared, and interspaced by a very
few black circles, chiefly in Brazil and the Argentine, but dotted at rare intervals round the great
half-circle of the north-western republics.

" I wish they'd put a key to this map," said
Peter, " it might have answered a lot of
questions."

" That would have made little difference to
you, gentlemen."

They both swung round. Alison stood in the
doorway, covering them with a heavy calibre
revolver.

Slowly they both raised their hands. Despite
himself, Peter shivered. In her eyes was the same
wild stare that they had seen at the dinner-table.

" You fools," she said quietly, " why did I
waste time arguing with Leopold; I might have
known he was right, we were bound to kill you in
the end. Why couldn't you stay sleeping while
the 'plane came. I didn't want to kill you, because
you came here by accident.   But you shall not

stop us. More blood will flow before it is finished;
what difference do two lives make? ''

It was Dandy who answered her. He had been
rummaging at the desk when she came in, and as
he turned he had stepped sharply away from it.
It dawned on Peter that by his doing so the girl
could no longer cover them both at the same time.

'' Why, Miss Alison,'' he said calmly, '' we do
seem unlucky in our meetings. Last time the intro-
duction was a rifle; now it's a revolver.'' He
laughed gently. A shadow of doubt crossed the
clear resolution of the girl's face as she turned her
eyes from one to the other.

'' I'm sorry about the coffee,'' Dandy went on,
and something about his attitude sent the hair
creeping on Clintock's spine. '' It was really very
good coffee, but——''

He sprang like a tiger. Even Peter, who was
expecting something of the sort, was taken by
surprise, and Alison was caught completely
unawares. There was a click as she managed to
pull the trigger once before the revolver flew from
her hand and she found herself held in the
same bear-like grip as José had that evening
experienced.

'' Don't struggle,'' advised Dandy, still gently.
'' I don't want to hurt you; but if you make a fuss
I'll have to. That's better,'' he added as Alison
ceased the fusillade of kicks on his shins '' Now,
Peter, get that length of cord out of the desk and
bring a chair.''

Quickly he forced the girl into the chair. " Get that lump of curtain and tear it into four," went on Dandy, and as Peter complied, they used the strips so that they could bind the girl clamp-tight to the chair without skinning her wrists and ankles.

" A gag, too," added Peter, " else the other's a waste."

" True," said Dandy, and fishing in his wallet pocket he produced a clean handkerchief.

" I was saving this as a little luxury for myself," he said, wistfully balancing the prize on his hand. " But, however——"

With a shrug he rolled the handkerchief and, removing his ham-sized palm from Alison's mouth, he fixed the gag, binding it in position with a hand-kerchief of Peter's.

The latter, as an afterthought, removed the scarf which the girl wore. It was a fair-sized square of that pickled-cabbage colour so popular among immigrants to Latin America. Clintock quickly bound it on his own broad shoulders and picking Alison's wide-brimmed hat from the floor crammed it on his own head.

" Camouflage," he said to Dandy. " Pretty passable at a distance in a searchlight. This'll be useful, too," and he retrieved the revolver, set the safety catch, and stuck it in his belt. " Let's put her behind the desk, so's she can't be seen from a casual glance." This they did, and then went cautiously to the front of the fazenda.

" Food," said Dandy, and crammed his pockets

full of the biscuits that still adorned the table.
Better still, there was a bowl of water, from which
they both had a quick drink. Dandy was in
favour of a few mouthfuls of boiled beans, a dish
of which had also been left; but Peter forbade.

"Enough valuable time wasted already," he
said.

But Dandy compromised by scooping a few
beans into the now empty drinking bowl before he
followed Peter out on to the veranda.

To their right they saw a couple of peons standing by the shed. To their left, tethered to the
veranda rail, was Alison's mare.

"Lord! What luck!" whispered Peter.
"Quick, you get up in front of me. She'll have
to carry the pair of us."

Peter untied the reins while Dandy scrambled
up in front of the saddle; then he swung himself
with the ease of a practised horseman, and set the
mare at a canter westwards round the hollow.

The peons, apparently, suspected nothing. For
a furlong they rode, expecting any moment to hear
the sound of pursuit or the vicious whistle of bullets
but none came.

Followed a nightmare ride that, had the stakes
been less, would have been ludicrous. Peter
hugged Dandy tightly to his bosom, gripping the
reins as best he could. This was necessary as
much to reduce the appearance of there being two
people on the mare, as to keep Dandy from falling
off.

Paget himself clung desperately to the pommel behind him with one hand, vainly trying to tip beans into his mouth from the bowl which he still held in the other. In all he got a couple of mouthfuls, the majority of the beans going right and left to the ground; in the end he flung the bowl away in despair.

Twice during the long mile to the path up the slope the searchlights from the far lip picked them out. But each time either the scarf or the horse was sufficient evidence of their *bona-fides,* for the lights passed on.

It was Dandy who spotted the path. In the moonlight the track was by no means easy, but he had remembered a huge boulder which lay just to the east of it.

"You'd better get down," suggested Peter as soon as they had got sufficiently far up the slope to be in the cover of the shrubs. "The nag's a bit blown." ·

"I wish I'd thought of wearing that scarf," grumbled Dandy good-naturedly as he slipped off. "Come on, old faithful."

The mare had not been slow to seize this opportunity for a breather, but a slap on her hindquarters from Dandy sent her off again.

In this way they scrambled up the slope, the mare often showing them the way where the rocky path was doubtful. They came abreast of the searchlight shed almost before they realised it. A voice hailed them out of the darkness.

" Paulo," Peter answered the question as to their identity, " and Juan is with me. His horse fell on the slope and broke a leg; is yours here; we have urgent orders?"

But this bold attempt at a second horse was evidently too much for the gods of chance.

" Paulo?" came the angry reply. " I am the only Paulo on this fazenda. Who are you? Stay where you are. Without waiting for Peter to reply Dandy scrambled on to the mare's back again, and they set off up the path beyond the searchlight.

" I'm glad he can't shine that light round this way," shouted Clintock as they left the infuriated Paulo behind, to the accompaniment of curses and a couple of shots loosed off into the dark.

" He'll set the whole pack of 'em on our heels," Dandy shouted back.

" Won't matter if we beat 'em sufficiently to warm up the 'plane's engines." Clintock spurred the mare with his heels.

They made the top of the rise, to find a small plateau rising to the east to the peak that they had first started out to scale, but sloping away to the south to the rounded edges of the valley in which they had landed the day before.

Now that the ground was level, Clintock put the mare into a gallop, and the heavily-laden little beast made gallant speed across the plateau.

Clintock headed her diagonally to bring them as soon as possible to a spot from which they could survey the valley. In a couple of minutes they were riding along the edge of the valley searching for a spot where the slope was sufficiently gentle to promise a descent without loss of speed.

Freeing a hand, Clintock pointed. A mile away the great wings of the '' Thunderbolt '' could just be discerned, glistening silver in the moonlight.

'' Last lap,'' he bawled to Dandy.

But in that very moment there came the flashes and pock-pock of rifle fire from the far side of the valley, and two bullets whined and ricochetted in the rocks below them.

From the distant ridge, nearer by far than they to the '' Thunderbolt,'' three horsemen galloped across the valley. Retreat to the 'plane was cut off.

CHAPTER TEN

GOMEZ IS SUSPICIOUS

CLINTOCK reined the mare in fiercely, and rode away from the ridge of the valley, where they were a skyline target in the moonlight. The precaution was none too soon. Evidently the riflemen on the opposite ridge had realised that their shots were falling short, for the next fusillade was nicely ranged, and passed uncomfortably close.

For a minute or two Clintock, nonplussed and chiefly concerned with getting out of sight of the marksman across the valley, let the mare have her head, and the animal retraced her steps at a brisk trot which brought them shortly to the top of the path up from the hollow.

The searchlights were gone when they eased up on the edge of the slope. Evidently the shots had convinced their operators that the fugitives were away to the south in the upper valley. But below them, on the path up which they themselves had so recently raced, they heard shouts and the ring of hooves on the rocks. Evidently Paulo had not been slow in summoning aid.

Clintock surveyed the ground to the west. It was open scrub, thicker than the heaths of the temperate zones, but with no trees that could offer cover to a horseman.

" Looks the only way," suggested Dandy.

But Clintock shook his head.

" We'd never make it," he said. " They could ride us down before we'd gone a mile. This nag's tired, and we're two up, while they are fresh. Even if we got a fair start, which isn't likely, they could shoot us down from here if they've got rifles."

The position seemed indeed desperate. Southward, cutting them off from the 'plane, they could catch the thunder of galloping hooves coming across the valley. Northward the men on the path were rapidly approaching the top of the hollow. To the west lay the prospect of a hopeless race across open country.

" Nothing for it but to chance going down the side of the gorge," said Clintock. " The horse is no longer an advantage, anyway."

They slid off the mare's back. Leading her to the top of the path, Clintock gave her a resounding slap that sent her slithering down the steep slope. The shouts and curses of the party below as the mare went scrambling and kicking into the middle of them came up to the flyers' ears as they doubled across the edge of the gorge.

" Keep as low as possible as you go over the skyline," warned Clintock. " That's the only place where the fellows on the other side are likely to pick us out."

Luck favoured them. The spot where they reached the edge offered the promise of a possible, if precarious descent. Thus saved from running along the skyline looking for a suitable place to climb down, Clintock and Paget were able to slip unnoticed over the edge and into the deep shadow of the gorge.

" Take it steady," cautioned Peter as soon as they were ten feet down. " We're in no immediate danger here, but if we send any stones down they may hear."

They listened. To judge by the shouts the party that had come up the slope were exchanging news with the horsemen from across the valley. Eventually they heard the riders spread out and make away to the west.

" They've formed a cordon," opined Peter. " They evidently think we've taken cover in the scrub. Now let's get on down."

In the gloom the rocky side of the gorge, which rose almost perpendicularly, was stiff going. But after one or two perilous minutes, and at the cost of skinned hands and bruised knees, half an hour found them a hundred feet below on the bed of the stream.

" Now," said Clintock, after they had had a breather, during which they both munched a few biscuits and drank from the swiftly running water, " which way shall we go?"

" They're almost bound to have left a guard on the 'plane," said Dandy, " and those fellows on the far ridge are a sight too handy with a rifle for my peace of mind. I vote we go northwards, and chance our luck in the hollow again."

" I think you're right," Clintock agreed. "They won't be expecting us there. If we can work our way round the hollow we might get away to the north. We've got easily six hours of darkness yet; we could put up ten or twelve miles between us and the hollow by dawn. Then we shall have to go to cover and carry on again to-morrow night. We'd have to go that way even if it weren't for Leopold and his pals, or else we'd get sunstroke."

" Where'll we head for?" asked Dandy.

Clintock shrugged his shoulders.

" That's in the lap of the gods," he said. " The big thing at the moment is to get clear of here."

So they set off down the gorge. They noticed the stream had decreased in size since the morning and Clintock observed that it probably only ran in the rainy season.

" That's one of the peculiar things about the Lower Valley," he said. " It drains such a small area, otherwise they could never have made the use of it that they have."

Presently they reached the end of the gorge and emerged into the moonlight again. The hollow semed as quiet and deserted as when they had first seen it. No trace of light or movement came from the buildings hidden below them.

" Evidently the whole staff is out looking for us," said Peter. " Which way round shall we go?"

" Toss up for it," suggested Dandy. But his humour fell flat. Far up the gorge came the ring of hooves on rock; someone was riding hard towards them.

" No rest for the wicked," cursed Dandy, surveying the bare rocks round them, for here the sides of the hollow were clear of scrub. " They do catch us in darned awkward places. Tell you what, Peter; let's follow the stream down."

" Better than nothing," agreed Clintock, " on you go."

They slithered the first eighty feet. It was hopeless to try and get a footing on the wet rocks; but they contrived to keep sufficient equilibrium to fetch up on the concrete block which Dandy had taken for a sluice. This turned out to be merely a solid dam, turning the stream eastwards into a narrow culvert. Along this they scuttled like a couple of tight-rope walkers.

Before they had gone a hundred yards the stream turned sharply and fell sheer for about ten feet, only to be checked and turned in its original direction by a second dam.

Dandy paused doubtfully on the brink.

" Have to chance it," urged Peter. " We're still visible from above, but there's cover down there."

It was no pleasant jump. The landing space consisted of a slab of concrete a foot wide and eight feet long, with the prospect of rolling head over heels down the remaining two hundred feet of slope if you overshot it.

Dandy went first and landed sprawling but safe.

He picked himself up just in time to steady Peter, who had landed clear.

The culvert now ran eastwards at a steady slope down between an archway of thick undergrowth, through which they scrambled, crouching. Before they realised it they were on top of the miniature waterfall. One more jump and a scramble and they were back behind the fazenda exactly where they had hidden an hour or so before.

Their first thought was to wonder if Alison had been found. The light was gone in the room in which they had left her, but creeping up the side of the fazenda, they heard voices in the room abutting onto the veranda.

" It's the two fellows from the 'plane," whispered Peter to Dandy. " Listen!"

Evidently the incident of their escape had not helped to clear up Lieutenant Gomez's doubts.

" My young friend," they heard his tall companion arguing, " these Englishmen are purely incidental. The Administrador has just telephoned that they have them trapped in the top valley. Their 'plane is under guard, and they are surrounded. As soon as it gets light they will be rounded up and shot, if not before. The Administrador is on his way back now, so that we can get off to schedule; that shows how much he is worrying."

" You say they came here accidentally," countered Gomez in a surly tone, " but I think they were spies."

"Spies?" the tall fellow laughed. "Then there were never two such thorough agents. These two, if you are right, my friend, went to England and joined the English Air Force. After ten years they come back here, flying to Pernambuco non-stop and getting themselves on the front page of the world's newspapers to ensure secrecy. No, lieutenant, these are no spies."

"But if they are famous there may be search parties?"

"True. But we have arranged to have them reported at suitable times over Bolivia and Jujuy. There will certainly be searches, but in the Andes of Chile, my friend, not in the Matto Grosso. We wrecked their flight because we had no wish to have hairbrained English careering all over Brazil just now. By pure mischance they came down on the very spot where they might do damage. You can't blame these people for waiting instructions before shooting them. Fortune has favoured these Englishmen just the once that any man is entitled to, but now they are finished. As I said, they are incidental."

"So," said Dandy, as he listened to the whispered translation of this, "we owe the holes in our tank as well to this outfit. Jolly little crowd!"

Clintock nodded.

"Come on," he said. "Let's get going."

But Dandy grabbed his arm.

"Peter," he whispered excitedly, "what fools

we've been. Trying to get to a 'plane two miles away with one on our very doorstep.''

He pointed to where the big tri-engined monoplane stood barely fifty yards away.

'' Probably fitted with self-starters,'' gloated Dandy. '' Full of juice and her engines half-warm. That's a better idea than a night trek north. Eh?''

'' O.K.,'' said Peter, '' we'll chance it.''

Stealthily they crept out to the machine; the door to the cabin was on the far side. Away to the east they heard a party of horsemen coming riding along the hollow, and as they ducked under the fuselage they heard Gomez and his companion coming out on the veranda to greet the returning party.

'' Quick,'' whispered Peter, '' here comes the Administrador. In you go, Dandy, and we'll just do it. Quick, man. Hurry!''

'' I can't,'' Dandy moaned, '' we're done, Peter. The door's locked.''

CHAPTER ELEVEN

OUT OF THE FRYING PAN . . .

CLINTOCK'S FIRST REACTION was incredulity. A
lock on an aeroplane door is very rare.

" Must be jammed," he said, shouldering
Dandy out of the way. " Let me try."

But the door responded no more to his tugging
and shoving than Dandy's.

" You're right, Dandy," Clintock stood back
and gauged the distance of the horses' hooves from
the east. " They'll see us if we try to dodge back."

" Half a tick," Dandy moved farther down the
fuselage. " There's usually a second panel on
these crates. Here, give us a hand."

Ten feet farther aft he had discovered the con-
tours of a lifting panel. The machine was designed
for general purpose aircraft, and this panel was
intended for loading emergency stores for rapid
transmission from a base to the front.

The second exit was a combination of a door and
push-panel, hinged at the top. A loose nut in the
bottom of the frame had stopped the flap from
going right home after the peons had unloaded the
'plane. With typical Latin nonchalance nobody
had thought of giving it a shove to.

Dandy had contrived to get his fingers under the
flap at one corner, and with Clintock's assistance
he soon had the panel open.

They scrambled inside, and gently pulled the panel home over the obstructing nut. The rear compartment into which they had gained access ran practically the whole length of the fuselage from the tail to the forward cabin, which was partitioned off.

As soon as he had taken in the lay-out of the machine, Clintock scrambled across to this partition, feeling with his hands for the means of opening the door into the forward cabin. The door was of the sliding type. To their dismay they discovered that this too was locked or bolted on the far side.

" Blast!" breathed Dandy on receipt of this information, " this is out of the frying pan into the fire with a vengeance. Shall we chance being heard and smash it down?"

" I doubt if we could," said Clintock.

" Well, what else is there to do?"

Clintock did not answer for the very good reason that he could think of nothing else.

But their indecision was not to last long. Outside, they heard the sound of footsteps; Gomez and the tall man had walked over from the veranda to the 'plane. They heard a rattle of keys and then somebody climbed into the cabin.

" So it was locked," breathed Clintock. " Better lie doggo for the moment. If they see us now we're finished."

" Just check up on the petrol, lieutenant," they

heard the tall man's voice from outside. " It should be about three thousand."

" Three thousand gallons?" whispered Dandy who had caught the word " petrol." " We must be going to the moon."

" Litres, you fool," Peter whispered back. " That's about seven hundred gallons. Enough for fifteen hundred miles, I should think. Phew!"

His mental picture of a huge circle with Lower Valley as its centre and a radius of fifteen hundred miles, was broken by a nudge from Dandy.

" There's the Administrador."

Sure enough, the latter's rough tones had entered the conversation.

" They've taken to the scrub to the west." He was answering a question from Gomez. " Don't worry, they'll be dead by this time to-morrow. Are you all ready. The lights should be on any minute now. It's just half-past two, so you're in plenty of time."

He had addressed the last half of his remarks to the tall man, and his voice had become deferential. Pressing his ear against the fuselage, Clintock could just catch an exchange of remarks between the two men, which was evidently not intended for Lieutenant Gomez's ears.

" How did the Estabracho business go?"

" Oh, that." The tall man's voice rose slightly in enthusiasm. " It went off perfectly. I forgot, I brought a paper for you. It must be in the back somewhere."

" It doesn't matter." The Administrador waived the suggestion of finding the paper. " I shall hear everything very soon now, eh?" He laughed a quiet, grating laugh then aloud he said:

" Here are the lights. A good trip, Excellency. Good-bye, Lieutenant. Remember me——"

Clintock lost the rest of his remarks in the roar as Gomez warmed up his engines. The roar subsided to a drone as the tall man climbed into the cabin and shut the door.

Through the chinks in the partition between them and the cabin the flyers caught the glare of the searchlights. They sensed the big 'plane taxi across the hollow and turn. The note of her engines rose, and they felt her run and lift. A moment later they were bracing themselves against the side of the fuselage as she banked, but they could command no sense of direction. A few minutes later they were settled down, speeding steadily through the night—to somewhere.

They gauged that dawn had broken by the increasing temperature. The gloves and coats that they had carried on their original flight had been left in the " Thunderbolt "; even overalls had been a burden in the ground temperatures of a Brazilian summer. But Lieutenant Gomez seemed to prefer high altitudes, and Clintock and Paget dozed half frozen during the four hours before the sun made itself felt inside the fuselage of the speeding bomber. They were torn between caution, which bade them keep well aft, and the attraction of the cabin heating which made itself felt beyond the light partition.

About seven o'clock the daylight began to filter through odd apertures from the forward cabin, and the interior of the 'plane was lit by the faint grey of diffused light.

" I reckon the sun's on this side." Clintock whispered, his hand on the starboard ribs of the fuselage. " It's noticeably warmer than the other."

" Going north—eh?"

" Looks like it. Ever seen this design of machine before?"

Dandy nodded.

" It's an adaption of a Hanworth-Strongley type. I saw one before they were delivered—that's what made me think of the loading panel."

" Where are the bomb sights?"

" Up in front. I remember thinking how hot it would be with that third engine."

" Is there a rear gun turret?"

" No. Her cabin guns cover the tail. I always reckoned that the type was under-gunned; but it's got a terrific climb, and a wicked turn of speed."

" Then there's no rear observation window at all?"

" I don't remember any. Half a tick, though. I believe some of 'em have a photographer's aperture aft."

He scrambled towards the tail and explored the floor with his hands.

" Here it is," he tugged. " Give us a hand with the cover."

" Gently," cautioned Clintock. " Does it slide or lift?"

" Slide."

" Well, open it about a couple of inches."

Dandy complied. Far below them lay a carpet of unbroken green. Even from that height it was startling in its intensity of colour, so level was it, without markings or limits, that it gave them the impression of being stationary.

" Open it further," whispered Dandy. " We can't see a thing through a crack like that."

" They might see the light from the cabin."

" Chance it."

Clintock nodded his agreement, and slid the aperture cover right off, revealing an expanse of squared glass about eighteen inches long and two feet wide.

They knelt on the side of the glass and gazed down.

" Over ten thousand feet I should say," ventured Dandy. " No wonder it was so cold. What is that—prairie?"

" No," Clintock shook his head. " It's jungle. The Matto Grosso; just mile upon mile of colossal trees and undergrowth so thick that it takes a day to cut through one mile of it."

" Crickey! Who lives there?"

" Only Indians, and mighty few of them. There are one or two established tracks through it, but the rivers are the only permanent means of travel. Between the rivers there's thousands and thousands of square miles, literally untrodden by white man.''

As they watched there crept across the glass a tiny silver snake, stretching as far as they could see from side to side.

'' Tidy-sized river,'' vouchsafed Dandy.

Clintock nodded.

'' Can you pick out any shadow?'' he asked. They both peered down.

'' Yes,'' Dandy pointed. '' On this side—see, there's a sort of marking line, while the other side's much vaguer. That'll be the shadow of the trees on the bank.''

'' Must be a good long shadow, to be so clear from this height,'' said Clintock. '' That means the river runs more or less north and south. By George, yes, you can see, it disappears where the bank turns out of the general direction.''

Then we must be going more west than north?'' said Dandy.

'' Must be.'' Clintock leaned back as the river passed from their view. '' Now I come to think of it, if we'd gone north all this time we'd be getting near the Amazon estuary! and due west would have fetched us up over the Andes. No doubt about it, Dandy. He's heading up north-west into Fawcett's ground.''

They watched a little while longer, but nothing

further appeared in the aperture to give them an inkling of their direction.

" Better shut it," said Clintock. " If nothing happens we'll have another look in half an hour's time."

He shifted back to give Dandy room to push the cover over, and as he did so his heels caught on something that rustled. He turned and picked up a newspaper.

" This must be the one they brought for the Administrador. Hold up, Dandy. Just leave enough light to read by."

Dandy slid back the cover to leave a half-inch slit, through which the daylight came in a beam. Clintock held up the paper so that he could see the front page.

" Good Lord," said Dandy in surprise. " It's in English."

Clintock nodded.

" It's the *Rio Tribune*," he explained. " It's a Yankee paper published in Rio. Keep your voice down."

Together they read: —

SHOT MINISTER—OUTLOOK GRAVE.

Tension is growing between the two Premier Southern Republics following the shooting of an Argentine Senator and member of the Government, Don Julio de Estabracho, outside his home in Palermo, uptown quarter of Buenos Aires.

The police claim to have pinned the assassination on Brazilian-born Manuel Rapelo, medical student, known to be of dubious political connections.

Rapelo alibies that a stranger put up with him the night before the crime, and this was the man trailed to his home by the secret police. The stranger, says Rapelo, subsequently fled to the docks.

His story is widely disbelieved.

The situation rapidly worsened when the local Intendente, delivering the funeral oration, referred to " Brazilian Outrages."

The Northern Representative has sharply protested and Argentine is now torn between the reasonable course of apology and reluctance to counter public feeling, which is running to unprecedented heights.

PAN AMERICAN CRACK UP?

Coming on top of the unexpected failure of U.S. mediation in the Transandine Railway dispute, the quarrel manifests a new setback to the President's policy of Continental Solidarity.

British and European comments—page 4.

" So," said Clintock when they had finished, " that is the Estabracho business. And it is going perfectly."

He looked at the paper again.

" Two days old," he said. " It must have happened the night we took off from Falmouth. Come to think of it, I remember Ellison saying something about the political situation when we landed at Pernambuco. I didn't pay much attention to it."

Dandy scratched his head.

" Do you think," he said slowly, " that these people engineered this?"

" It certainly looks that way."

" Then—shooting us up must have been just a sideline?"

" Evidently. I told you the fellow up the front was at great pains to assure Gomez that we were mere incidentals."

Dandy continued scratching.

" Then," he asked, " what's the connection between the two. Why?"

" Search me," Clintock's sardonic face broke into one of his rare smiles. " Maybe we'll know by nightfall—if we live that long."

CHAPTER TWELVE

. . . AND WELL OUT

ABOUT AN HOUR LATER they passed over a range of hills.

" If only we had a map," yearned Clintock, as he gazed down through the aperture, and marked with a wet finger on the glass the approximate direction of the sun. He consulted his watch, and by the same crude method performed the requisite geometry over the squared surface of the window.

" A few points west of dead north-west," he reckoned, surveying his handiwork. " He must be heading for Peru."

" It's all the same to me," Dandy philosophised.

For twenty minutes the hills provided a change in the landscape below them. Then the green of the jungle flooded out the browns and greys, so they shut the window because there was nothing more to be seen.

It was a quarter-past nine when Clintock woke Dandy, who was dozing against the side of the fuselage.

" Dandy," he whispered, " he's throttling down."

The drone of engines had dropped several tones.

Discarding caution in their curiosity they hastily uncovered the aperture.

The 'plane was at a much lower altitude than when they had last looked. Twisting gradually below them as they circled lay the fork of a river and its tributary. Across the tongue of land at the confluence straggled a town of one-story buildings, some in stone, some of wood. Behind these lay a wide plain, in the centre of which stretched what they took to be a huge natural fault in the rocks, having from the air the curiously regular appearance of a five-pointed star. The sun caught something at the centre that glistened like a leaping flame.

" Here we go," said Dandy, as the monoplane banked steeply and her nose went down.

Gazing through the tilted aperture they caught a glimpse of a half-circle of hills, girding the landscape to the west and north, where the plain ended abruptly in a steep scarp. Beyond the two rivers receded an unbounded vista of unbroken matto; but within the huge triangle between the rivers and the scarp, not a scrap of green could be seen. Only the sprawling ramifications of the star spread black and mysterious around its gleaming centre to break the dead even grey of the plain.

" Queer sort of rock formation," said Dandy. " Are those terrific rock faults or what?"

" No," said Clintock, puzzled, " they're flat. Look, there are men running along one of the points. Gracious, man! There's a wind sock."

At the centre of the star, they could now see, was a huge building, the walls of which rose sheer from the surrounding plain, and from a staff on one of these ramparts a wind sock hung limply.

" Home from Home," said Dandy. " I wish the welcome committee was out for us."

Clintock nodded grimly.

" Put the cover over," he said quietly. " We're getting a bit too low to look out any longer, they might spot us."

Dandy obeyed.

" Let's get as far back as we can," Clintock said quietly, as outside the engine roar fell farther. " He's coming in now."

They crammed themselves as far back as the construction of the fuselage would allow.

Lieutenant Gomez was no mean pilot. He brought the heavy monoplane gliding in to a perfect landing. Clintock and Paget scarcely felt the shock of contact with the earth, and the complete cessation of motion was the first certain indication they received that they were down.

They caught a jabber of voices forward. Five minutes passed, and then the engines picked up again. They felt themselves moving forward.

" Crikey!" whispered Dandy, " don't tell me he's come all this way just to drop in for a chat."

" Shut up," said Clintock, " we're taxi-ing. This must be the smoothest air field in the world."

" And the biggest," added Dandy after a pause.

Minutes passed, and still the 'plane went on.

" He's landed on the wrong continent," commented Dandy. " It's getting devilish hot here."

" It'll get hotter," surmised Clintock. " Unless my compass calculation was wrong, we must have come well up towards the equator. Hallo. We seem to have arrived."

Once again the 'plane came to a standstill, and this time the engines were switched off. More voices followed from the cabin and they heard the sound of movements on the ground. Anxiously they strained their eyes towards the panel, the first chink of daylight through which would mean discovery.

But evidently the storage space in the big monoplane had completed its usefulness when it was emptied at Lower Valley, for no one came to disturb them. Complete silence reigned around their hiding place.

" I bet they're going to leave us standing in the sun," gasped Dandy, mopping his forehead. " Just our luck."

But he was wrong, for not long afterwards they heard the ordered tread of a body of men marching in step. Came the shout of orders, but in an unknown tongue.

" Beats me," Clintock told Dandy in a whisper. " They must be soldiers of some sort, but the drill isn't in Portuguese or Spanish."

" I said it." said Dandy wryly. " We have flown to the moon. You see it was gallons of petrol, not litres. Whoops!"

His wit was cut short by a series of jerks following a succession of encouraging shouts.

"They're wheeling us somewhere," surmised Clintock.

A moment or two later they felt the temperature inside the 'plane drop.

"Out of the sun," breathed Dandy. "Thanks be for small mercies."

From outside they heard more orders. And the pad-pad of obedient feet. The ground squad formed up and marched off.

"I must say I admire their discipline," Dandy observed. "Wheeling this crate must be a heavy job, yet nobody uttered a word except, presumably, the sergeant."

"I've got it," said Clintock, suddenly. "Indians! Of course, that explains the ground squad being so mute. Ordinary peons would have jabbered like a pack of monkeys."

"Indians or not," said Dandy, "they know how to man-handle a 'plane."

"You've said it," Clintock nodded in emphasis, and fell to musing.

The inside of the 'plane was now in complete darkness. For an hour they waited, shifting from one position to another in their efforts to keep comfortable.

"This is getting on my wick," said Dandy at length. "What do you say to a look round."

"It 'ud be better to wait till nightfall." Clintock urged. "No sense in taking risks now."

" We run just as much risk staying here,"
Dandy argued. " After all, it's quite on the cards
that his 'plane is due to be loaded up this afternoon,
at any rate overhauled; then we'd be trapped.
Outside we do stand a fighting chance, especially
if we get the hang of the lie of the land."

" Uh," said Clintock, unconvinced.

Dandy stuck the darkness for another half-hour.
Then he started off on his theme again.

" Another thing, Peter. Suppose the people at
Lower Valley find some clue as to where we've got
to. It's by no means unlikely."

" Lower Valley must be over a thousand miles
away," said Clintock.

" I know; but these people seem to have a pretty
good system of communications. Must be short-
wave wireless, I'd say. They might get on to here
and ask them to cock an eye over the 'plane just
for luck."

The darkness and the continual sense of being
cooped up had played even on Clintock's iron
nerve; he could not deny that there was a good
deal of sound reason in Dandy's arguments.

" O.K.," he agreed. " Let's chance it."

They wriggled over to the panel. Gently Clin-
tocq braced his shoulder against it. It came open
with a break-away that sounded to the keyed-up
flyers like a pistol shot.

Clintock paused and they listened intently for
the shout that would announce that someone had
spotted the panel opening. But they were alone;

Clintock shoved the panel still farther and pushed his head round.

" Coast's clear," he whispered, " come on."

He scrambled out, and Dandy followed. Clintock carefully closed the panel and gazed round.

The hangar into which they had been wheeled was lit by a beam of sunlight filtering in from the roof. The building surprised them by its spaciousness; the big monoplane was amply accommodated at its entrance, and farther back they caught the lines of at least two more machines. The walls were of terrific stones and rose to a height of some thirty feet. The roof was in sharp contrast and consisted of a rough lay-over of long, half-trimmed tree trunks interlaced with a sort of thatch of planks and boughs and a sprinkling of corrugated iron.

But it was the door that attracted their immediate attention.

It was a solid structure of some sort of bronze work.

" My hat," Dandy surveyed it in amazement, " it must weigh a couple of tons at least. I bet it slides. No hinges that you could get up here would hold that lot."

" No," said Clintock grimly, " and no force that we'll be able to bring on it will open it, even if there's no sort of locking device."

Dandy looked around.

" Half a tick," he said. " We aren't trapped for all that. I bet we can climb up there."

He pointed to the wall beside the door. The huge stones dovetailed together with a nicety that was astounding, but in the corner the series of protruding edges made quite an easy climb. Dandy leading, they scrambled up. Where the roof crossed over the door, which they could now see was fully half a foot thick, there was a clearage of about ten inches.

" Whoever built this place," observed Dandy, as Peter scrambled up beside him, " had a nice eye for massive architecture. The design is simple enough, but the execution must have been terrific, and none too recent, I fancy. These stones are well weathered."

They gazed out. A mile away to their left, shimmering in the heat, lay the western of the two rivers, making the fork they had seen from the air. To their right the dead even plain stretched away for about three miles to the building on which they had seen the wind sock. Its brown vista was split nearly the whole way by a wide band of gleaming black.

" Basalt, or something of the sort," opined Clintock. " I wonder how it was laid. It's as smooth as glass."

" I reckon it was uncovered by digging," said Dandy. " See, it's about six feet lower than the rest of the plain. Probably the whole area has a strata of the stuff under the ground layers."

Ahead of them they could see the river trailing away towards the hills which bounded all the horizon. Between them and the steep scarp they had noticed from the 'plane, was a collection of buildings and several huge tanks. Only around this could they see signs of movement, but they could not see details, for the buildings were a good five miles off.

" Across to the river is our best chance," said Clintock, when they had surveyed the landscape. " Once we got across we'd have perfect cover 'til we made the hills. That must be at least ten miles."

" Always wanting to go trekking round the countryside, you are," Dandy groaned, " and now in wet clothes. I vote we hang around here, we might get another chance at a 'plane."

" More likely get half a dozen bullets," said Clintock. " We can't get the 'plane out of here without sliding this door open. If you've got any ideas on the subject, I'd like to hear 'em."

" True," said Dandy. " I suppose you're right. But the scheme doesn't offer any prospect of food, and I'm hungry, Peter."

Clintock shrugged his shoulders.

" We have to plan for the hour at present," he said. " Here's the remains of the biscuits we pinched at Lower Valley. We might as well eat now as not."

He glanced up. A cloud had passed over the sun, and the relief from the intensity of the glare was very noticeable. As far as they could command it, the south-eastern horizon, which was mainly blocked out by the huge walls of the hangar, was full of lowering black clouds.

" Storm coming," he said, and nodded in confirmation of his own judgment as a gust of hot wind swept suddenly across the plain. " Shouldn't think this roof would stand up long to tropical rain. I wonder if they cover the 'planes at all?"

" I wouldn't be surprised," Dandy agreed, his mouth full of biscuit. " There's some big canvas sheets behind the 'plane we came in. I wondered what they were for."

He blew a mouthful of crumbs sharply into the wind.

" Not only a storm coming up," he grimaced. " Look."

In the distance, where the great black band of smooth rock was narrowed by the perspective, a squad of men had appeared from behind the centre building, and was marching steadily towards the hangar.

CHAPTER THIRTEEN

THE PIRANHAS

" Easy," Clintock restrained Dandy, who was already preparing to wriggle through the open space above the hangar door. " They can't get here for the best part of an hour at that pace; and if we climb out here they may spot us. Try the roof to the side there."

Maintaining with his toes a precarious hold in the division between the two top blocks of stone, Dandy worked his way along the side of the hangar wall for about five feet. Here he stopped, and shoved at the roof near the join with the wall. As Clintock had surmised it was held there chiefly by its own weight, and when he had joined Dandy, the two of them, shoving with all their might, managed to lift one of the rough planks sufficiently for Clintock to get his forearm underneath.

" Quickly," he gasped, for the dead weight on his hand and wrist was terrific. " See if you can force your way through."

Dandy wriggled headfirst into the narrow opening. Clawing the wall he dragged himself outside, turned on his back and, holding the overlap of the roof he contrived to draw first one leg and then the other through the opening.

Had the roof been smooth the exit would have required almost impossible feats of balancing; as it was the axe-trimmed timber offered very good handgrips and Dandy was able to brace himself until he could grope down with his toes to the same footholes as they had used inside. Thus poised he took the weight of the plank they had dislodged, while Clintock edged through in similar style. And then they both worked from block to block down to the ground.

But it had been slow going, for one slip would have meant a fall to the iron-baked surface of the plain, with a sprained ankle, at least, as the result. By the time they had got their breath, a cautious look round the corner showed that the approaching squad of men had covered fully half the distance to the hangar.

" They're trotting," said Dandy, " they've spotted us."

" Not they. They'd be coming a darn sight faster than that if they had. It's more likely they want to get here before the storm breaks."

Clintock stood back from the corner and surveyed the ground between them and the river. The distance, he confirmed his previous reckoning, was fully a mile. The terrain was dead level, and not a single shrub or boulder offered the slightest cover. To his left the hangar was revealed as the last of four or five similar buildings, all of the same massive construction, and tremendously long, giving them the appearance of narrowness, though in actual fact they were wide enough to take the wingspread of all but the very largest of 'planes.

Between each was an open space of about a couple of hundred yards. The whole effect gave the impression of a mighty wall rather than a series of buildings.

All this he took in at a glance. For a moment he debated whether it would not be better to try to follow the line of cover of the buildings, but reason told him that the chances of their crossing more than one open space unnoticed, was small; moreover, the line of the buildings followed the curve of the river, and there was no likelihood that they would be any better off at the far end than at this.

" Straight across, is the best, I reckon," he said to Dandy. " If we keep in the line of that peak there, we shall have the hangar between us and them all the way. Half a minute."

He pulled Alison's revolver from his belt, and wrapped it quickly in his handkerchief, which was smothered in the grease he had wiped from his fingers after his vain attempt to adjust the " Thunderbolt's " compass.

" Might as well keep it as dry as possible," he said, and opening his shirt he pushed the oily bundle inside his singlet, afterwards buttoning both shirt and overalls up to the neck.

" That'll hold, I think." He patted his bulging chest. " Ready? Come on, then."

They started out across the open space at a smart double.

A mile is a very easy distance to bandy about in print, but to run it, even under ideal conditions, is no mean test of a man's physique. Here the conditions were by no means ideal. The ground was as unyielding as rock, their clothes, light as they were, seemed to cloy their every movement, and above all there was the overpowering swelter of the tropical day.

Grimly they plodded on, the sweat oozing in dirty rivulets from every pore, breath coming in aching gasps.

" Stick it," shouted Peter to Dandy, who being of shorter stride and carrying more flesh, suffered the worse. " We must be nearly half-way."

" I'm — doing — fine," Dandy panted.

Another hundred yards thudded beneath their feet. Clintock turned for the first time to glance over his shoulder, and as he did so he heard a shout from the middle of the line of buildings and a group of men came running.

" Spread out," warned Clintock, for he had seen the men kneel on the ground and he guessed what was to follow. " Keep a good distance between us, and run like blazes!"

Even as he spoke the first bullets whined above their heads, followed by the pock-pock of the rifles.

" Don't bother to dodge about," shouted Dandy, for Clintock had changed the line of his run, " just run."

A splendid shot himself, he realised that the range was long and wanted gauging to a nicety, and that the shimmer from the torrid ground would spoil the most accurate of sighting.

His contention was borne out, for in the next ten seconds a whirlwind of fire churned the earth on all sides and split the air above them but nothing came near enough to be dangerous.

Volley after volley followed, and as they neared the river the fire broke out from immediately behind, indicating that the party they had first spotted had come on the scene and joined in the hunt.

The moment before they made the river bank the storm burst. A flame of lightning cleft the heavens from horizon to horizon and the wind rose to a shrieking gale. A curtain of drenching rain swept across the plain with the speed of wild horses. In a moment the world was one howling, tearing mass of driving torrents.

"Our luck's holding," gasped Peter, "keep your shoes on—you'll need 'em on the other side."

And with that he plunged into the rain-churned water, closely followed by Dandy.

The river was here about a hundred yards wide and the current fairly slack. The flyers were not expert swimmers, and, exhausted as they were after their long run, their clothes dragged like lead weights.

"Best foot forward," Clintock puffed alongside Dandy, "we've got to make the other side before they come up."

In opening fire while Clintock and Dandy were

running their pursuers had made a fatal mistake. Of necessity, this kept them stationary, thus giving the two airmen an invaluable start, without which they could hardly have made the river crossing before the others arrived on the bank, in which position the flyers, being in the water, would have presented a sitting target.

As it was, only a bare ten feet separated them from the bank when the pursuit hove into sight. The driving rain was against their faces, and panting men do not make good marksmen, otherwise Dandy and Clintock would have failed on their last lap. The vicious chuck-chuck of bullets sent the water flying menacingly close. As they dragged themselves out a round went " phut " in to the earth in the foot or so between them.

But a second or so later they were ploughing into the thick undergrowth that came down to the very edge of the river. Bullets tore and slashed at the greenery round them, but the shooting was haphazard now, and they were temporarily safe.

Dandy flung himself down and doubled over his clasped hand.

" I must have a blow," he groaned. " I couldn't make another inch. Not even—ooch!"

He sat up sharply, his stitch forgotten. From his calf he tugged with an effort a little chubby fish and flung it away.

" By Jove, that hurt!" he panted. " I felt something cut me like a knife just before the beggars opened fire."

He stared down ruefully at his leg; his overall was stained with a growing patch of blood. He pulled out his handkerchief, and hitching up his trouser leg, he bound up the half-inch slash which was then exposed.

" Come on." He struggled to his feet. " We can't hang about. What's the matter?"

Peter was staring after the fish he had thrown away. " We don't need to hurry," he said slowly. It was Dandy's turn to stare.

" Don't what?" he gasped. " Have you gone crazy?"

Peter shook his head. " That was a piranha," he voiced his thoughts. " The bullets must have scared off the rest of the swarm." He whistled. " That was mighty close."

" What was?"

" Come and see." Peter answered, and to Dandy's amazement he commenced picking his way back towards the river. Dandy followed, wondering.

Once more on the bank, they gazed cautiously through the verge of the undergrowth.

Four or five of their pursuers had taken to the water, swimming strongly on their sides, holding rifle and bandolier above the water.

" Come on, Peter," Dandy tugged anxiously at Clintock's sleeve, " we're wasting time. They'll be across in a minute or two."

" Wait," said Clintock, and there was a grim edge to his voice.

The leading swimmer was practically half-way across when the man behind him suddenly yelled and, dropping his rifle, rolled over. There was a flash of silver as he struck out wildly with both his arms and legs.

A jabber of voices went up from the bank. One man, evidently in command, shouted to those in the water. To Clintock and Paget his voice was lost in the wind and rain, but the effect on the swimmers was electric. All but the leader abandoned their rifles and ammunition and turned back for the nearer bank, striking out with as much splash as possible.

The one man who had not heard the warning kept steadily on. The flyers watched fascinated. Of a sudden the water round him was churned with a flurry that was not caused by the rain. The man's head rose as though a sudden weight had dragged his legs under. His cries rose above the storm, the pitiful shrieks of an animal in distress, calling on deaf fate for mercy, and knowing there can be none.

He fought madly, drifting in the slow current; gradually the turning, heaving mass lost the shape of a man. Scarlet streaked out across the mud-brown water. Sickened, Dandy turned away.

" Heavens!" he said, his voice reverent in awe, " let's go, Peter."

As they turned away Clintock caught Dandy's arm and pointed. " The last act, I think."

Down the stream came what Dandy had taken

for a couple of logs. But they were drifting faster than the current. They neared the still struggling soldier: came a sudden gleam of teeth and a snap like a whip-crack. The logs sank in a red-streaked swirl, and with it the last of that mass of pulp that five minutes before had been a human being.

"We owe a devil of a lot to this storm breaking," said Peter with a grimace. "Come on."

For a solid hour they fought their way through a mass of tangled tendrils laced with spider's webs. Nothing moved in the jungle, but there was always the silent menace of the unknown.

As soon as they came to an open space Clintock halted and took out the revolver. The handkerchief was soaked, but the weapon itself had not suffered too badly. He wiped it with loving care, taking out the five precious rounds of ammunition the magazine held and drying each separately.

" If they're well made they'll have taken no harm," he said, and tested the mechanism of the empty gun. " Seems to be O.K."

He reloaded and put the revolver in his belt where it was handy.

A little later they struck a rough sort of track, much overgrown. This they followed and, the going being easier, they made good speed.

Towards midday the storm eased up as suddenly as it had come, and sunshine came filtering down between the mass of trees above them.

In the heat of the day they struggled on,

obsessed with the idea of putting as many miles as
possible between them and the river.

" Peter," said Dandy suddenly, " I don't feel
too good.   My head—it's swimming round,
round."

He staggered, and Clintock caught him and
lowered him to the ground.

A cursory examination proved his fears well
founded.   Dandy had a touch of sunstroke. What
with the exertion and the heat, not to mention the
ducking, it was to be expected.

The country they had now reached was more
open, and he dragged Dandy across to the shade of
the nearest tree.   There he knelt, supporting his
comrade's head.   He gazed round at the blank wall
of forest that surrounded him.   Enemies behind,
the unknown for miles in front, without supplies,
without even food or water, and with a sick man
on his hands his plight was desperate.   A wave of
despair, product of exhaustion and lack of food,
swept over him.   He fingered the butt of the
revolver speculatively.

Even as he made up his mind to fight the
unbending fates to the last ditch his ears were
assailed by that peculiar cross between a hiss and
a whistle which is the universal method of attract-
ing attention in Latin America.

Twenty feet away a curtain of creeper had
parted, to reveal a chubby, nut-brown face dis-
tinguished by a tousled beard and a very bright
pair of eyes.

CHAPTER FOURTEEN

SCRUBBY

"CHE," called the face, "Ché!" and then persuasively, " put down the shootin' iron, 'tain't noways needed."

For Clintock had jumped to his feet and levelled the revolver.

" You come out," said the airman cautiously, " and let's have a look at you."

The creeper swept aside, and a stocky, powerful man stepped into the clearing, ramming a battered hat on his cropped head.

He had the appearance of being in the forties, though his beard was streaked with grey. Around his waist was slung an amply-filled bandolier and at his hip a long-barrelled revolver. His clothes were stained with travel, and consisted of riding boots, voluminous trousers, reminiscent of bombachas, and a short bottle-green coat in the Spanish style. His open neck shirt revealed a powerful chest.

" You ain't got nothing to worry about, ché," he said to Clintock as he came up. " I bin trailin' you the last hour or more. Why, I could ha' picked you off any time I had a mind to."

This, Clintock realised, was perfectly true.

" I'm sorry," he said, and thrust the revolver

back into his belt. " I'm just a little nervy at the moment."

" Why, certainly," the newcomer dismissed the matter with a smile. " It wouldn't be in nature if you wasn't. I guess you just broke away from the outfit yonder? "

He jerked his thumb back towards the river. Clintock nodded.

" I heard the shootin'," continued the stranger, " and I thought I'd come away down and see what was on. You been around this joint long?"

" No. As a matter of fact, we only came this morning."

" In that 'plane I saw over, I guess?"

" The same," said Clintock.

Dandy groaned and stirred.

" Why," said the stranger, " here we are chatting and your partner's in trouble. What's the matter with him?"

" He's got a touch of the sun, I'm afraid," said Clintock, kneeling again by Dandy's side.

Quickly, and with the air of constant use, the newcomer bent down and felt Dandy's pulse. Then he pressed the palm of his hand against the unconscious man's forehead and inside his shirt on his chest and back.

" Sure has," he said, straightening up. " 'Tain't serious, though. Kin you carry him? There's a stream away over thar."

" I think so," said Clintock and, stooping, he picked Dandy up in his powerful arms. Holding

the sick airman like a baby, he staggered after the
stranger, who seemed to know his way about.

For about a hundred yards they pushed through
the undergrowth, and then, passing under another
curtain of creeper, they came to a series of steps
hewn in the rocky soil. Down this they went, and
turned into a little grotto, on the far side of which
ran a sparkling rivulet.

" Put him down thar," said the stranger, and
Clintock obediently lowered Dandy beside the
flowing water.

" Hold his head and shoulders up," said the
older man and, cupping his hands, he flung the
water up over Dandy's face and head.

The water, Clintock noticed, seemed icy cold,
and under the cover of rocks and creeper the grotto
was cool in comparison with the swimming heat
outside.

Very soon the treatment had effect, and Dandy
opened his eyes.

" I'm sorry, Peter," he murmured slowly.
" Feet—feet just wouldn't go."

Consciousness flooded back to him, and he sat
forward from Clintock's knee.

" Where the ——?" he started, but the
stranger pushed him gently back.

" Take it easy, pard," he urged. " Feel better
now? Well, just turn over and dip your face in
the water."

Dandy did so, and then sat up.

" Who's our friend?" he asked Clintock as he

rubbed his dripping hair with his sodden hand-kerchief.

Clintock laughed.

" Why I don't really know," he said. " It's time we introduced ourselves."

" Sure," said the stranger. " The name's Boulder—Scrubby Boulder they call me. Shake, partner, I certainly am pleased to meet you."

" Not half as much as we are to meet you. My name's Clintock, Peter Clintock, and this is Dandy Paget."

" Dandy—huh?" The stranger's eyes twinkled. " Why, that sure does seem appropriate."

And they all laughed, for Paget looked anything but his nickname, with his crumpled clothes, wet hair, and a couple of day's growth of whisker.

" You come from the States, don't you?" asked Clintock, for Boulder had the easy, rolling accent of the South.

" I certainly do," confirmed the latter. " Lee River, on the borders of Virginia and North Carolina. I don't suppose you know it?"

Clintock shook his head.

" I'm afraid not."

" What part do you fellers come from?"

The flyers were nonplussed. Most Englishmen, born in such a small and homogeneous country, are not birthplace conscious.

" Well——" Dandy ventured, " London, as much as anywhere."

" You don't say!" Boulder seemed amazed.

" Y'know, it's certainly funny: most of the English I've met in South America came from Scotland," and he roared at his own joke.

" Have you been here long?" asked Clintock.

" About a week. I've just finished settling in, as you might say."

" Know anything about the place across the river?"

" Not a thing, son. And I certainly am not impressed with your reception."

" Nor were we," said Dandy grimly.

" I was prospectin', you know," Scrubby confided. " Nothing in particular—just prospectin'."

" Alone?"

" Sure. Ef you make a strike there ain't any sharing, and ef you don't—why a crowd wouldn't help any."

" I was on the Plate one time," he went on, " but it's a worked-out situation down there, so I kinda drifted north into Bolivia by easy stages. An' then I came clean across to try my luck in Peru. But I didn't get on so good. There was guys back there who thought nothin' of me, just nothin.' Jealous, I guess, so I packed my kit an' left."

Clintock grinned.

" You found Peru too hot, maybe," he suggested.

" Why, that's just about right," Scrubby

nodded knowingly, " too hot by half. Here,
now, a guy has room to move."

" What country is this?" asked Dandy,
interested.

" Why, I shouldn't be too ready to guess."
Scrubby pushed his hat over his eyes and rubbed
the back of his head.

" But you must know what country you're in,"
said Dandy, amazed, and Clintock laughed.

" He always thinks of frontiers as they are in
Europe," he told Boulder, " with fortifications
and miles of barbed wire."

" Sometimes they're that way here," said
Scrubby, " leastways, I have seen them. But
most times it's a mountain or river or something.
But up in this part they ain't so hard and fast.
Each maps 'em according to their own fancy and
leaves it at that. And there's a heap of sense in
it," he added, " 'cos it don't matter a cuss either
way within fifty miles or so. I reckon we're in
Brazil, if you ask me, unless we're further south
than I think, then maybe we're in Bolivia. I
haven't struck a township in three weeks—not
since I left the mountains."

" Brazil?" said Dandy.

" Sure. Acre Territory or the Amazon
Province."

Dandy whistled.

" Why, the place is the size of Europe," he
said.

" And then some," observed Peter. " But, as

Scrubby said, what the devil does it matter?"

" I don't know," said Dandy doggedly, " a fellow ought to know where he is."

They fell silent for a few minutes. Then Boulder got to his feet.

" If you feel better, pard," he addressed Dandy, " I guess we'll get going. Our friends way over may have a boat or something, and they sure seemed reluctant to lose your company."

" I'm fine," said Dandy, getting up.

" Come on, then," said Clintock, and he started back to the steps.

" Not that way," Boulder halted him, " there's a better way than that. Keep close behind me."

They followed him along the bed of the stream. The grotto followed a deep fissure in the rock and ran winding on, it seemed, indefinitely. Sometimes they passed under natural archways of rock, and once Clintock thought they had gone clean into the hillside, but they emerged again, and picked their way over the rocky bed of the stream, beneath a thick ceiling of undergrowth and an impenetrable tangle of creeper with bright yellow flowers.

It was late afternoon when they eventually came to a halt.

" Here's my camp," Scrubby told them.

The grotto opened out into a small enclosed valley. Around the stream were a couple of acres of thick lush grass. A horse was cropping it, and as they came forward he lifted his head and whinnied.

" Not a bad animal," said Scrubby. " I picked him up on the coast for a few dollars. He was half starved, poor crittur, but I nursed him a bit, fer I had it in mind to shift out at the time, and you can't carry enough food on your own back for these trails."

He patted the horse affectionately.

" Go and have a look at the view," he suggested, " while I get supper."

They walked to the far end of the valley which he had indicated, and scrambled up on to an outcrop of rock.

They had expected to be well in the hills, for the half-underground path they had followed had been a steep gradient most of the time, but the view they commanded took their breath away.

Below stretched a long sweep of rock-strewn hillside, disappearing into the thick green of the jungle which lapped at its foot like a sea. Across this turbulent carpet of green they could catch the glistening water of the river that had so nearly been their grave. Beyond, the plain spread out like a map, with the great black star in the centre.

The spur of rock commanded the whole scene southward to the tumble of huts and houses at the river's confluence right across to the steep scarp which terminated the plain to the north like a rampart.

They could see the building in the centre of the five roadways across the plain, and even at that distance it looked massive. Between this and the scarp they saw the buildings they had spotted from the hangar, with the line of great round structures so suggestive of tanks. Nearer, they could pick out the line of buildings following the curve of the river, looking more like a wall than ever in that perspective.

And on all sides, coming right to the edge of the gigantic V formed by the two rivers, was the jungle. Eastwards and southwards it stretched into the misty distance, but within the containing limits of the two rivers not a tree was to be seen.

" This place gives me the creeps," said Dandy, " who could have cleared all that land so perfectly or built those terrific walls up here away from civilisation? It's like a dream, Peter."

Clintock pursed his lips.

" There's only one explanation," he said slowly. " It must be Indian work."

" Indians?" Dandy laughed. " Don't be daft, Peter. Why, these Indians are terrifically backward, I remember reading somewhere. Blowpipes and that sort of thing."

" That's right up in the Amazon basin. Here we're in the heart of the old Inca Empire. You know, the people the Spaniards fought against. It's been in my mind ever since we landed; now I'm sure of it. This must be the last stronghold of the Incas, the secret city that Colonel Fawcett lost his life trying to find."

" But——" Dandy expostulated, " where are

the Incas now? What has it got to do with shooting Ministers in Buenos Aires and secret flights across the country in pinched 'planes?"

" I'm hanged if I know," confessed Clintock, " but it's the only feasible explanation of those buildings."

He broke off, for they heard Scrubby's cheerful voice hailing them from the valley behind.

" I have only one straw left to convince myself I'm sane," said Dandy as they clambered down from the spur of rock, " and that's the fact that I'm darned hungry."

CHAPTER FIFTEEN

IS IT AN INCA ARMY?

THEY FOUND SCRUBBY seated at the mouth of a fair-sized cave. He had kindled a fire with a stock of wood piled just inside the entrance. Using a peeled stick as a spit, he was roasting the carcass of a bird about the size of a chicken.

" Sort of quail," he told them, " only larger. There's quite a few of 'em round here. This mornin' I was lucky, and managed only to wing one. You can't keep anything you shoot during the day—goes off like that. But if you can get one down alive you can build a sort of cage out of rocks and your supper keeps itself."

" 'Twon't be long," he said, " they cook quicker over an open fire like this."

" It smells just wonderful," Dandy said. " I've only had one square meal in four days, and I wasn't allowed to keep that for long."

" How come?" asked Scrubby.

" Why this way," commenced Dandy, and he sketched a rough outline of the events leading up to their arrival.

Scrubby listened without comment. Once or twice Dandy paused, half expecting the little bearded man would doubt him, but Boulder kept his eyes on the sizzling bird, nodding slightly from time to time to show he followed the sequence of events.

" This woman you mention," he said thoughtfully, " you said her name was——"

" Alison," Dandy repeated.

" Her second name, now," asked Scrubby. " Would it be—Sorsarelli?"

" I don't know. She said her father was a Brazilian. She's not very tall, with red hair and very blue eyes and a terrifically firm jaw."

" Why," Scrubby chuckled a deep, throaty chuckle, " you certainly do seem to have an eye for detail. I did think it might be some one I once ran across on the River Plate. She was a Porteña, though."

" Alison is an American—very much so," laughed Dandy, and he related the incident at table, which he had omitted in his previous story.

" You don't say!" Scrubby raised a pair of bushy white-flecked eyebrows. " She said just that—huh?"

" Yes. Funny sort of thing to come out with, eh?"

" I've heard ideas of the same sort expressed before," Scrubby said, holding the bird up for his closer inspection. " Down by the coast now there's a heap o' young fellers with no work worth while that talk that way. Running round with banners and that when thar ain't no election on."

He shook his head in condemnation of such practices.

They sat silent for a little while, and the setting sun flooded the little valley. Then Scrubby said:

" What d'you make of the joint over thar?"

" Gives me the ' heebee jeebees,' " said Dandy.

" You ain't the only one," Scrubby told him.

" I don't reckon you've noticed, but the matto between here and the river, now. Thar ain't a thing bigger than a spider movin' in it. In a week I haven't seen as much as a blamed lizard. And Highball there,"—he indicated his horse—" he's happy up here, sure enough, but the first time I tried to get him down thar he just refused. Wouldn't budge an inch. That sure made me cautious. In Virginia, now, when we say horse sense, we mean just that. And the Injuns, too, I had a pair of trappers with me back on the trail that I picked up in the Andes. They was almighty glad to sling along of me 'till we got within fifty miles of this place. Then one night one of 'em asked me what direction I was heading the next day, an' I said ' north-east.' And sink me if the beggars didn't just fade away in the night. Yet they didn't pinch a blamed thing. Say what you like, pard, that ain't in nature, no, sir!"

" But," protested Dandy, " there are Indians over on the plain. And Peter reckons the place was built by Indians."

" You seen 'em?" asked Scrubby sharply.

" Have we not," said Dandy with emphasis, and he filled in the details to his previous account of their escape of the morning. " One of the blighters put a bullet within a couple of inches of my ear. And those pir—what's the word, Peter?"

" Piranhas."

" Well, they evidently aren't afraid of the hoodoo on this place. Nor are the alligators."

" Fish ain't flesh and blood, leastways not in the same way as a man or a hawse, now," said Scrubby seriously. " But you was telling, pard. There's Injuns over the river?"

" Yes and darned well disciplined ones. Beats me!" said Dandy.

" It shouldn't," said Scrubby. " Did you ever go to one of your own colonies, son?"

" I went to India when I was first commissioned," said Dandy. " Why?"

But Clintock caught Scrubby's meaning. He whistled.

" A native army—eh?"

" Sure looks like it," Scrubby nodded. " Why not? These Injuns, now, they certainly don't look much, but have you never read about the heap of trouble they gave the Dons when they came up from the coast?"

" That's true enough," said Clintock. " And those buildings lining the river. I'll swear they were built as forts."

" Forts?" said Dandy, still incredulous. " Even supposing they had the means to build 'em, which they wouldn't have had, why should they build forts up here?"

"Huh," said Scrubby disdainfully, "you certainly wouldn't talk that way, son, if you'd been to Cuzco. The Inca Washington as you might say, now. And down thar there's a blamed great fortress place by name of Sachsahuaman. It wasn't new when the Dons came, by hookey, but it sure is the cat's whiskers. I've seen the forts erected by Uncle Sam at the Golden Gate. As good as U.S. engineers could make 'em, and that sure is pretty good. But this Sachsahuaman, now— why, our forts are like kids' toys compared with it. And that certainly was put up by Injuns. What they had to fear, search me, but when those guys fortified a place, buddy, it stayed fortified, I'm telling you."

Clintock nodded in agreement.

"I stand corrected." Dandy crossed his fingers in mock fear. "I hope I don't get sent to bed without any supper."

Darkness had fallen with tropical suddenness. Presently Scrubby announced that the bird was done. The three of them sat round and tore the carcass with fingers and teeth. Scrubby produced a packet of the same type of hard unsweetened biscuits that had featured so prominently in their diet at Lower Valley, and they filled out any creases left by the bird.

After they had finished, Scrubby pulled a foul, little pipe from his trousers' pocket, filled it with the blackest tobacco imaginable, and sat ruminating, puffing great clouds of tobacco into the still night.

" I reckon," he said at length, and very slowly and deliberately, " I reckon we're all kinda curious about this joint across the river."

Clintock and Paget agreed.

" I ain't wantin' to force you," said Scrubby. " You got the means now to hit the trail. It's a fair step to any place human, I sure must admit; but we could make it easy enough in, say, a coupla weeks or three."

Clintock cut him short:

" Plenty of time for that," he said, " if you think we can knock up enough grub."

" Sure," said Scrubby calmly. " Leave the larder to me, pard. I'm used to lookin' after my little self."

" Well, then, perhaps we might form a sort of alliance. And when we've satisfied our curiosity we could make our way back to the coast."

" Why that's the very thing I was half of a mind to propose." Scrubby clapped his thigh. " Are you on, partners? Split the profits, share the risks."

" Count me in," said Clintock and Paget together.

" Why then," Scrubby continued, " I propose we have a good night's sleep an' in the mawning we'll work out a plan of campaign. How d'you like that?"

" Suits me," said Dandy, yawning.

" O.K. then; let's turn in."

Scrubby stamped out the fire and carefully spread handfuls of earth over it.

" Funny how habits sticks," he said. " I always did cover my trail."

He led them inside the cave. For about forty yards it ran back, and then, turning, it dropped away sharply.

" Looks like a mine," observed Dandy.

" Probably was," said Clintock, " if our surmise about the rest of this place is right. The Indians were great miners; they covered temples with gold and gems."

" Easy up." Scrubby reached out a hand in the darkness and stopped them. " Sure am sorry thar ain't no illumination, gentlemen, but fortunately we have a few sheep hides. When in Rome do as the Romans do, I say."

The hills in which this valley lay were not high enough to make the night cold. So the three men stretched themselves on the skins and composed themselves to sleep.

Dandy was the first to drop off, and soon Clintock followed. But for long into the night Scrubby sat, his back against the side of the cave, his pipe glowing like a little lamp in the darkness, lost in his own reflections.

CHAPTER SIXTEEN

RECONNAISSANCE

THEY WOKE just after dawn. The cave was full of cool sunlight; on the far side Scrubby was busy with a cairn of stones.

" Just caching the stores, pards," he explained, " we might be away for two or three days."

They went over and found, cunningly concealed beneath the stones, a veritable warehouse.

" Yeah," Scrubby agreed, " I sure did load Highball up. Nothin' of the noble spirit of adventure about yours truly, gentlemen. I'm for comforts all along the line."

Half an hour later, having washed in the stream, Dandy announced his enthusiastic support of this policy. For Scrubby provided them with a breakfast of maize pancakes and coffee served in a tin with all the savoury ingenuity of a man who spends his life in the open.

Over breakfast they debated their next move.

" Suppose we follow the river up to its source," suggested Clintock, " then we could get across without a boat."

" I doubt if that's possible," Scrubby drawled. " This stream, now, is maybe a hundred yards wide here, yet according to the landfall it don't rise above twenty miles away. I ask you, partners, that certainly ain't in nature."

" You think there's a gorge through the hills away up there?" Dandy indicated the north-west.

" No, sir; my private computation is that this river comes out of the hills a full-blown affair. 'Tain't nowise unusual."

" Then you think we could get clean round this circle of hills?"

" Sure," Scrubby nodded. " Come up to the top of the valley, and I'll point out just what I'm figurin' to do."

Once more on the spur of the rock, they surveyed the plain below, still half-hidden in morning mists.

" I see it this way." Scrubby pointed to the steep scarp that formed a barrier across the open side of the great V made by the two rivers, " that thar line of rocks slopes away to the east. Get me? And of itself it ain't anyways so high as this side of the half-moon."

" I see," said Clintock. " You think that from here the whole range gets lower and gradually peters out to the north-east."

" Sure. Now if we make an early getaway, gentlemen, we could make the far end of that escarpment by sundown. Keeping half-way down the ridge the going ain't that bad, and it wouldn't be above fifteen miles or so."

" And we'd get a closer look at those buildings at the far end of the plain from there," Clintock concurred.

"Why, certainly; and then I reckon we'll find the slopes easier, and we can come down at our leisure on the right side of the far river."

"True enough."

"And what certainly appeals to my humble imagination, gentlemen, is that if our friends way down there are that anxious about your welfare to come and look for you, it's on this side that they'll look; and that, partners, is just where we will not by any means be."

"Good enough," said Dandy. "It strikes me as being a jolly bright idea—all but the fifteen miles walk."

He cast an eye longingly at Highball, who was passively cropping the grass by the stream.

"Pity we don't have two more of 'em," Scrubby followed his glance, "but it wouldn't be an advantage to take him. One hawse between three, partners; why it just don't go. He'll look after his little self, I guess."

The question of transport thus settled, there only remained the apportioning out of the load of food Scrubby insisted on taking and they started north-eastwards along the shoulder of the range of hills.

The going was even better than Scrubby had predicted. Every now and again the hillside was scarred and pitted with longwise slashes.

"This beats me," said Dandy. "It's different from any rock formation I've ever seen."

"I'm not so sure that it is just rock formations." Clintock surveyed a long even shelf of rock. "I think all the strata round here are volcanic, but these faults are too regular. I'd rather think they were workings of mines or something of the sort. What d'you say, Scrubby?"

" Why, certainly," said Scrubby. " If these guys dug for something up here they sure must have built some roads. I happen to be a Republican myself, but the original citizens of this country, why, public works were the breath of life to 'em."

" That's dead right," said Clintock. " The Incas built a highway into each of the four provinces of their empire and you can still trace them."

" Well then," Dandy said complacently, " I'm very much obliged for the trouble this lot took."

As the morning wore on each successive vista that chance turns of the hillside gave them of the plain below, showed the western of the two bounding rivers coming nearer and nearer to the hills.

About an hour before noon they struck what was unmistakably an overgrown pathway. Great blocks of dressed stone had been sunk into the hillside, giving a firm carriageway some ten feet wide, running north-eastwards round the half circle of hills.

They had hardly gone a mile along this relic of ancient culture, when they came above the spot where, faithful to Scrubby's prophecy, the river poured a turbulent torrent from a fault in the hills. The pathway narrowed suddenly and culminated over a titanic ravine in a small bridge. This was built of wood and stone! Originally massive in structure, it had settled with years and now presented a dubious prospect of extremely precarious old age.

After a short conference, they decided to risk the bridge. Scrubby, being the lightest, went first. He trod gingerly forward inch by inch, while the flyers watched him, heart in mouth, casting occasionally an anxious glance at the glistening arch of water, a sheer five hundred feet below. After he was safely over, Clintock shuffled carefully across. Either his greater weight or the continuation of the strain, gave the superstructure of the bridge a sickening sway.

" This," said Dandy, the heaviest, and left on the far side, " is the worst yet. My favourite nightmare, in fact."

He laughed without conviction, then squaring his jaw he took the bridge at a rush.

It was the last straw. Came an ominous sound of wood parting up, and from the path he had just left a huge block of stone tilted and went slithering into the abyss.

" Quick, Dandy," Peter shouted.

But Dandy needed no urging. He made the last six feet of the sloping bridge like a rocket, and turned breathless to see the remains of the bridge go twisting down into the river. For a moment the full extent of what had happened did not dawn on them. Then Scrubby said calmly.

" Waal, gentlemen, that certainly puts a long path between us and our camp."

" There must be a way along the top," suggested Dandy.

" Sure," agreed Scrubby, " but I don't fancy yours truly as a mountain goat. No, gentlemen, I can't see us getting back in such an all-fired hurry. However, as Lincoln said, ' Tackle things in due course and no sooner.' At the moment I propose we push on."

" Suits me," said Dandy, looking ruefully at the splintered end of the bridge, " but I don't share your high opinion of the Inca highways department, Peter."

Leaving the bridge, they found the pathway climbed gradually higher as they followed the range of hills.

" That's understandable," said Clintock, when Dandy commented on this. " We're getting round to the scarp at the end of the plain, so it would be practically impossible to build a pathway along the hillside there."

For an hour or more they lost sight of the plain on their right and clambered up craggy defiles which time and streams had cut into the solid rock. Gradually the pathway faded again, and as they progressed still farther the last vestige of scrub and grass disappeared.

Eventually they came out on to a bare plateau. Northwards the hills undulated away to another higher range some fifty miles off. Southwards the rock face fell vertically like a wall for three hundred feet, to make the scarp they had observed the day before.

They rested in the narrow shadow of a mighty boulder and ate dried meat and biscuits. Then at Scrubby's suggestion they advanced along the edge of the scarp till they found a niche where they could stretch full length and survey the plain below at leisure.

From where they lay, the buildings which had attracted their curiosity were about a mile to the east. At first glance they seemed to differ little from that in which they had been unknowingly confined when they landed, except that these were rather more square, and instead of being in a line stood each one behind the structures that in the distance had reminded them of tanks.

" And tanks they are," said Clintock. " Look, you can see there's a sort of aqueduct running between the near two and the end building.

" Wouldn't hold much," objected Dandy. " That stonework can't be more than ten feet high. Admittedly they cover a fair ground area, but——"

" They're probably sunk," said Clintock, " like the ones they have in the Australian bush. The tank itself may go as much as fifty feet into the ground."

But Dandy was not satisfied.

" Why have tanks, anyway," he objected, " With two healthy rivers within easy reach?"

" Drought perhaps. A lot of fair-sized rivers will dry up in a bad season."

" Huh. Then why have your tanks right bang in the middle, as far as possible from either river?"

For answer Clintock craned farther forward.

" Look," he pointed triumphantly, " I thought maybe that was it. There's a stone aqueduct running right to the scarp. There's your reason. This rock must be non-porous; it makes a colossal natural reservoir. We know there's water running in it because of the river higher up——"

" Exactly. The river *higher up*. That would take practically all the water from the surrounding hills."

" Well, if it isn't a water storage plant, what is it? Here, Scrubby," he turned to the little Virginian, " you don't seem to be saying much; what do you think?"

Scrubby, his eye fixed on the debated buildings said quietly:

" I kinda reckon your both right. It's a natural reservoir we're sittin' on, and those sure are tanks —or that's what they've turned 'em into. But not for water, no siree."

" Not water—I don't follow!"

" Smell, son. Go on, smell, smell hard."

They both sniffed the breeze.

" I can't smell anything," said Dandy, " except, yes, a sort of niff of road-mending, or diesels, or——"

" Yes!" burst out Clintock. " I've got it! Oil!"

" Just that." said Scrubby in the same quiet voice. " I've seen land in Bolivia so full of oil that the Indians scoop it from the puddles to light their lamps."

" But—" Clintock wrestled with the possibilities of the new situation, " but then, those buildings—you aren't suggesting that they're a refinery, are you?"

" Why not?"

" But it's impossible, up here—miles away from anywhere."

Scrubby shrugged his shoulders.

" Those tanks are built of the same sort of stone as everything else round here," he pointed out. " Kinda argues that the original inhabitants tapped and stored the crude oil for some reason or other. If it's a high grade strike it wouldn't need more than a ton of machinery, maybe. That sure wouldn't worry our friends to transport—huh?"

" I suppose not," Clintock agreed reluctantly. Then he added, " No wonder the General had plenty of fuel."

" Sure. I guess it's just what they wanted this end."

Clintock nodded. Then he cocked his ear suddenly. " Quick," he ordered, " get back against that overlap."

Round the range of hills from the west was coming, at a low altitude, an aeroplane.

CHAPTER SEVENTEEN

IT SHALL BE THE DAY OF THE RETURN OF THE SUN

THE 'PLANE roared overhead, some two hundred feet above the three crouching men.

"Hold steady," cautioned Clintock, when it had passed, " ten to one they'll come back."

" I doubt it," said Dandy with sudden conviction. " Did you see them take off?"

" No. Did you?"

Dandy shook his head.

" So what?" demanded Scrubby.

" I'm not sure," said Dandy, " but it struck me there was something familiar about her. I didn't see her properly, but suppose she had come up from the East without our noticing. After all, we were all concentrating on the ground immediately in front of us."

" You mean she was on a cross-country trip, huh?" asked Scrubby.

" I mean more than that," said Dandy. " Wait."

They all three watched the vista of plain and sky which the gully they had hidden in commanded.

" There," said Dandy triumphantly, as the circling 'plane came into view, " it is; I'll swear it!"

" Well, I'm blowed!" Clintock took the words out of his mouth, " the ' *Thunderbolt*!' "

Now that they could see her properly, there was no mistaking the familiar lines of the great monoplane in which they had travelled so far.

" That your ship—huh?" Scrubby followed the implication of their remarks.

Dandy nodded. " I wonder who flew her up from Lower Valley, with the compass all cock-eyed?"

" Somebody who knew the landfall between there and here," surmised Clintock. " She could have made it all since dawn. Keep down; she's coming back again."

But this time the " Thunderbolt " circled short of the scarp, on the crest of which they were hidden.

" She's going to land," said Dandy, and they all craned forward.

The big monoplane made yet another circuit and then came gliding in, but not as they had expected, along one of the great black roadways leading to the building in the centre. Instead, she landed at the north end of the plain, almost in front of the three men.

" Grandstand seats," commented Dandy, as the 'plane went taxi-ing away to come to a standstill in front of one of the buildings by the oil tanks.

" And nicely done," added Clintock.

" A sight better than yours at Lower Valley. Aha! And look who did it!"

In the clear air there was no mistaking the little figure that clambered out of the cockpit. Even at that distance they could distinguish the flaming red hair, and another purple scarf. It was Alison.

"That the party you mentioned last night?" Scrubby asked Dandy, and wriggled to the edge of the cliff to get a better view.

"The same," said Dandy. "It looks as though they've discovered where we got to."

"In that case, partners," said Scrubby, "I vote we shift on. Nothin' like keepin' on the go when there's folks anxious about your pre-cise location. I've had some."

They put his suggestion into effect, retiring a quarter of a mile from the edge of the scarp to make sure of being out of view. After they had been moving for half an hour, the sound of engines revving down on the plain sent them scuttling in search of fresh cover. But no further machine came scouring the barren plateau for them, and when the sound of engines gradually died away, they decided that it was probably the " Thunderbolt " going across to the distant hangars.

They pushed on, and as the sun was dipping towards the hills they had left, they found that the plateau swept down in a long, rolling slope to the river which bounded the far side of the plain.

After a careful survey, Scrubby, voted the expedition's scout by common consent, returned and reported the coast to be clear. Here was by far the most nerve-racking part of their long circuit of the plain. The open slopes offered little prospect of cover from any person coming from the direction of the enemy headquarters. At Scrubby's suggestion they made the remaining three miles at the double. The little Virginian himself set the pace with a steady, loping stride.

"Phew!" gasped Dandy as, their object reached, he flung himself down beside the bank. "Running about all over Brazil—you'll be the death of me!"

He turned over and plunged his head and hands in the river to cool himself, only to draw back with a cry of disgust. "Hullo!" he said, "what's wrong with this water? It stings, and it tastes foul."

"Huh?" Scrubby came over beside him and, cupping his hands, took a cautious sip.

"I'll be doggarned!" He spat it out. "Another Rio de Vinagre!"

"Rio—" Dandy screwed his brow in mental activity, "I've got it—River of Vinegar?"

"Sure. Way up on the Orinoco thar," he waved his hand vaguely northwards, "there's a river in those parts runs acid from something in the soil, and I kinda reckon on this is the same thing."

He tugged a piece of dried meat from the package in his side pocket. Cuting this in half, he threw the pieces into different parts of the river. They watched the two hunks of meat rise to the surface and go floating steadily down stream, unmolested.

"No piranhas hereabouts, I reckon," said

Scrubby. " Kinda useful observation, partners; gives us a sure fire avenue of retreat on this side."

He settled himself comfortably and yanked out his pipe.

" Might as well hev a smoke, fellers," he smiled. " Don't reckon I'll get one to-night."

And so they passed the hours till sunset. Dandy slept unashamedly; Clintock dozed, and Scrubby placidly smoked. Only once Clintock remarked that there were no insects near the river as might have been expected

" Huh," said Scrubby, and spat contemptuously. " Thar's a heap of power in good Virginian tobacco, I guess."

As soon as darkness enfolded the plain, they broke their temporary camp and moved on.

" We got a coupla hours, I'd reckon, before the moon rises." Scrubby eyed the eastern horizon dubiously. " We'll have to get places before then, partners."

They proceeded cautiously in single file for a mile or more along the river bank, until they had reached a point from which they could see the whole plain. Southwards there were lights and movement in the distant village. By the hangars and in the centre all was silent and deserted. One or two solitary lights suggested there was still somebody by the oil tanks. Scrubby pointed to these.

" Thar's our best line of advance, partners," he

said. " Anyway else they cin cut off our retreat if we're discovered."

" True enough, Scrubby," Clintock agreed. " And we can get there keeping along the bottom of the cliff. I don't fancy cutting across the open."

They skirted the base of the rising scarp westwards for a distance of some two miles. As they approached, they spotted a couple of horses tethered in front of the lighted building. This, they observed, was bigger, and stood at the end of the others.

" That's probably their headquarters this end," opined Clintock. " I dare say we'd find out a good deal of what we want to know if we could get in there."

Scrubby, at his own suggestion, went forward to survey the enemy position. In a quarter of an hour he was back.

" Ain't bad going, partners." He rubbed his hands, his eyes gleaming. " And that joint sure is a miniature information bureau. Right now, if you ask me, there's a council of war proceeding."

Following the wily little Virginian, the two airmen crept from point to point under cover of the still night, and finally fetched up against the wall of the end building.

Here, as before, they found to their advantage that the windows were paneless, but in the more confident atmosphere of the secluded plain, the occupants had not even bothered with a covering of sacking.

At a long table in the room they could plainly see the tall, erect man who had flown with Lieutenant Gomez the previous day. He was in earnest conversation with a broad-backed, dark-haired fellow, whose face was turned away from them. But by far the most striking thing about him was the fact that, in contrast to everyone else they had seen since leaving Pernambuco, he was cleanly and neatly dressed in a lounge suit.

Clintock and Scrubby, who whispered his knowledge of Portuguese, approached the window, while the now useless Dandy was left on guard at the corner of the building.

'' But, my dear General ''—the tall man's voice was the first they caught—'' there have always been risks. You can't play any game with stakes as high as this without taking risks.''

'' Nevertheless,'' said the man with his back turned, '' I fail to see why I should jeopardise the whole organisation because your people are in a hurry. I've built this thing from the start. It's cost me three years and more money than I'd care to count.''

'' And we have helped you.''

'' I don't deny it. Your assistance has considerably widened the scope of my plans. But the present time is anything but good. The slightest hitch would bring the United States Navy south like a hurricane.''

'' Yes. And what then?'' The tall man leaned back and adjusted a rimless monocle in his eye.

" Nothing. They would just hover off the coast—outside the three mile limit—and look silly."

" So you think."

" I know it." The tall man slapped the table in emphasis. " We have sixty million allies in the United States, General. They don't know it. They'd be insulted if you suggested it. Brave people, cool, hard thinkers, and steadfast in action. The sort of people who would sweep us back into the Atlantic if they ever got going." He waved aside the other's protest. " Oh, you can talk as much claptrap as you like in Santos and Lima, but here we are making executive decisions. We can't afford to believe our own lies, General."

The other man's voice rose in anger.

" Then it proves what I say. I dare not strike now."

" Just the reverse, General. You must strike now or never. These Americans, I say, are our unwitting allies. They are the people who see in us no threat to their own wealth and security. The mother who would not part with her son. The lover who cannot bear to leave his sweeheart. They are only too willing to let their politicians delude them. They would fight to the death without a moment's hesitation on their own doorsteps, but not here because they do not see that it is the same thing in the end. And they will cry out against unnecessary militarism; heed our propaganda; refuse to move themselves and clog the whole mechanism of state by their own simple honesty.

We shall be pilloried on paper, General, but not a shot will be fired until it is too late. But if you hesitate; if a breath of certain knowledge leaks out, one unwise act might turn those very allies into your implacable enemies. We should withdraw. We would do what you thought best."

The monocle glinted as he leaned back.

" If not the United States, then Britain," said the man addressed as General. " Do you forget the British interests in the south?"

" I forget nothing, my friend. I do not forget that Britain would not strike in China, in Europe. Besides, we have everything on our side. The trouble-maker always has."

" You mean the West Indies?"

" Precisely. We can stir up enough trouble there to last Britain a month—that's all you'll need, General. But once let an inkling of your plans out before you have a *fait accompli* and you are done."

The man with his back to them buried his face in his hands.

" I am half persuaded," he said at length. " The Gomez family are very influential. They will force the Defence Committee to hold an enquiry into this latest crash. It is the third in two months."

" Exactly. And now you have two crazy English that your men can't shoot. Time is your only enemy, General."

" Very well." The other rose in his decision. " It shall be now. The Day of the Return of the

Sun. That will suit the Indians better. Don't doubt my resolution, Excellency."

" I!—Doubt? Caution becomes a man of high decision, General." The tall man clapped his companion on the shoulder. " In years to come, we'll drink to this day."

The General nodded. Now that his decision was taken, authority had returned to his voice and bearing.

" We'll make it a National Holiday, Excellency," he laughed, " and now you really must get some food."

He turned and for the first time Clintock could see his face.

It was Ramon da Cuyta.

CHAPTER EIGHTEEN

DEDUCTIONS

CLINTOCK stood motionless for fully a minute after da Cuyta had dowsed the lamp and followed the tall man from the room. The full import of what he had heard was still dinning in his brain.

From the front of the house he heard the clamp and clatter of horses' hooves die away in the distance. He turned, and in the faint light he could see Scrubby stroking his beard, lost in reflection.

It was Dandy who woke him to life. The chubby airman came bounding along from his position on the corner.

" They've gone," he announced. " Did you hear anything?"

" Yeah," Scrubby told him, " he certainly did."

And between them they gave him the gist of the conversation between the tall man and da Cuyta.

" Old da Cuyta—eh?" said Dandy. " Well, I'm blessed."

" Say," Scrubby asked, " how do you two come to know that guy's name?"

Clintock told him.

" Waal," he remarked, " now that sure is a step forward, partners. That other guy looked familiar, leastways I figure I've seen his picture in a paper."

" That's funny," said Dandy, " I thought I'd seen him before somewhere. What did you make of the bit about the crashes?"

" I didn't," Clintock confessed.

" I was wondering," said Dandy. " Those 'planes we saw over the other side in the hangars——"

" What about them?"

" Well, I didn't see them properly but I fancied they were Marvoias——"

" They were," said Clintock. " I remember thinking that at the time."

" Just before we came away," Dandy went on, " I remember seeing a report on that 'plane. The Chilean Government had a consignment of six, and two went west in a week; I don't remember the details——"

" Why, of course," Clintock snapped his fingers. " If they just pinched 'em—naturally they'd be reported as crashed."

" Hi-jacking 'planes—huh?" Scrubby rubbed the back of his hand in his beard. " Say what you like, partners, this outfit sure has smart ideas."

" You've said it," Clintock jumped on to the sill. " I'm anxious to see a few more of them."

They followed him through the window. From somewhere in his baggy trousers, Scrubby produced a small electric torch. A cautious sweep of its beam revealed an ancient iron cupboard underneath the table.

" Sure looks the most promising start, partners." Scrubby bent down and examined the lock. "Hold this durned light."

He fiddled with the inside pocket of his coat, eventually to extract a length of thin steel wire, which he bent into a loop, and inserted in the cupboard lock. For two or three minutes they watched his gnarled fingers gently manœuvring the wire in the tiny circle of light. Came a faint click, followed by the more solid sound of steel falling on steel, and the door swung open.

" Fallin' off old logs," gloated Scrubby. " I've known 'em take half an hour."

He fetched a pile of papers from the old safe and put them on the table. Dandy held the torch while Clintock and Scrubby bent to examine them.

They were chiefly accounts of stores and equipment. Name after name passed before their eyes; some familiar, some unknown: oil, ammunition, small arms ammunition, aeroplanes, machine-guns, rifles. Men at this place, available storage elsewhere. Despatches, too, were included. An order to be at Lower Valley by noon on the 22nd addressed to an unknown name. Advice of the arrival of 'planes: the despatch of stores. Reports on the available strength of every air force in South America, with comments on their distribution and efficiency. Advice on the orders placed in Europe and the United States for warplanes. Lists of officers' names, and a plan which more detailed scrutiny revealed to be analogous to the Establishment publications of an army list.

"Waal I'll be done brown," said Scrubby, as he picked out document after document and handed them to Clintock for his opinion of their contents. "This sure looks like first rate organisation."

"Too good for my liking," said Clintock. "What'll we do with this lot?"

"Put 'em back," said Scrubby after a moment's thought. "If they find they're missing it'll queer our start back to the coast. And besides, there's certainly an advantage in knowing a thing or two without their suspecting. Hey! What do you make of this?"

He had opened a small drawer at the back of the safe, and from this he drew the one document it contained. It was a plain sheet of paper, with a message typed on it in cypher. Underneath this was printed what was evidently the de-cyphered message. And beneath this again, line for line, was a rough pencilled translation into Portuguese. it ran:—

"*Your observations noted. Despite this, action must definitely take place before the end of January.*

It is essential that all centres develop action in concert.

This organisation cannot undertake the strain of prolonged operations.

A second failure may involve undesired external consequences. It is of first importance that the

*character and source of our support remain for
the present unrevealed.*

" So." Clintock put the despatch down. " I
bet a quid that's what they were arguing about."

" Sure thing."

" Well that solves another query." Clintock
pointed to the second line of writing—the original
de-cyphered message. " There's only one country
where that language is spoken to my knowledge."

He handed the paper to Scrubby for confirmation.

" I sure would give five thousand for the original
of that," said the little Virginian quietly.

" So would any intelligence service," said
Clintock.

Scrubby looked at him sharply.

" Yeah," he said dryly. " The most interestin'
thing about this little love note, now, is it's
tone——"

He pointed again to the tell-tale line of tran-
scription. " Here's the guy that's giving the
orders—get me?"

" The ' organisation ' that is trying to help?"
Clintock nodded. " I bet they are."

He took the paper back from Scrubby, weighed
it in his hand, finally to fold it and put it in his
pocket. " I just can't bring myself to leave that
behind," he explained.

" O.K., partner." Scrubby shrugged his
shoulders. " Let's have another look around."

They examined the rest of the room, but all else was bare. Only on the wall hung a similar map to the one the flyers had seen in the Administrador's office at Lower Valley. But beneath each of the little circles there hung a tab with a number printed on it.

"What d'you reckon these are?" asked Dandy, turning one of the tabs in his fingers. "Indicators of some sort. Perhaps where each of the keymen are, using number instead of names."

"No," said Clintock. "There are two here with 5 on. Did you never go to the Air Ministry?"

"Once," confessed Dandy, "for my first interview. Why?"

"I wonder you've never seen this sort of thing before. They're 'planes, man. The numbers show the machines stationed at each place."

"Crickey!" Dandy whistled. "They must have—" mentally he added up the numbers on the tabs—"they must have five hundred 'planes."

"Not entirely," Clintock corrected. "Look, the ones in black are the regular machines of the various governments, and the ones in red are these people's. You can see that from the distribution."

Scrubby stepped close to the map.

"Ithi Caru," he read. "That'll be this outfit, I reckon."

"That's it," said Clintock. "I've been trying to think of the name all day. That's the name the Administrador mentioned."

"Waal," drawled Scrubby, "you'll be in-

terested to learn, partners, that there's sixty-two
'planes around these premises.''

" I can believe it,'' Dandy nodded. " Those
hangars would hold all that and more. But they
can't have pinched all that lot, Peter.''

" I don't suppose they have. You forget that
they have influential friends who might—shall we
say—loan them a squadron or so. Maybe that's
what can't afford to wait.''

" Thar's a heap of reason in that.'' Scrubby
agreed. " It 'ud give 'em just the whip-hand
around here that that sheet of orders indicates. You
remember what the guy with the pane of glass in
his eye said ' We shall withdraw. You can do
what you please.' ''

" And not only 'planes,'' added Clintock.
" What about the small matter of the bombs at
Lower Valley. They might conceivably have been
made on this side of the Atlantic, but I doubt it.
What do you think, Dandy?''

His companion shook his head.

" Never on your life,'' he said. " They didn't
seem at all the style of bomb I've seen before. And
practically anything made officially here would be
a copy of our types or the American. I'd remember
any of them like a shot. But anyway, it adds
another reason for the hurry. Deterioration must
be a big problem with stores in this climate. What's
eating you, Scrubby?''

The little Virginian was studiously measuring
distances on the map with his thumb.

" I figure," he ruminated. " that this joint can't anyways be beyond a latitude of 10° south."

" No," said Clintock following his measurement with his eye, " I should say nearer five. Why?"

" I was just worryin' my mind about this day these two guys fixed on."

" The Day of the Return of the Sun?" said Clintock. " I wondered what you'd make of that."

" Why, this way," Scrubby stroked his chin. " I was figurin' it 'ud be an Injun Fiesta. You remember he said it would please the criters. Waal, all these original citizens were obsessed with sun worship. I met a guy once in Bolivia who claimed he'd find out how old a temple was by observing a ray of sun falling on a stone."

" Hey!" said Dandy, " that's what they do at Stonehenge."

" Come again, partner?"

" It's a ruin on Salisbury Plain in England. By George! Peter," he turned to Clintock, " I told you this place gave me the creeps. I couldn't think what it reminded me of then, but now I do. Remember the time we went to Stonehenge at midnight?"

Clintock nodded.

" I've seen a reconstruction of Stonehenge, and it's not unlike that place in the centre. But go on, Scrubby."

" Waal, I can't say about this Stonehenge o'

yourn; but I figured maybe it would be the day when the sun was dead overhead again."

" Again?"

" Sure. Up here you get the sun overhead sometime before midsummer and then again after."

" I see, go on."

" Waal, it don't fit. If our computation of the latitude is correct it 'ud be March before the sun was overhead here. And those guys aim on kickin' off before January thirty-one."

" Maybe it's some other place." said Dandy.

Scrubby eyed him dubiously.

" Like this: When the Declaration of Independence was signed it was, perhaps, July the thirteenth in California, but you have to pick on one day, if you follow."

" Durn my hide!" Scrubby turned to the map. " It'd be Cuzco, o' course. That 'ud be their religious headquarters. And there the sun 'ud be overhead at the end of January. Blamed smart, you thinkin' of that, son."

" I don't often blossom out," Dandy commenced modestly, " but——"

He stopped short.

From across the plain came the clatter of hooves.

CHAPTER NINETEEN

TEMPLE OF FIRE

" Stay here," Scrubby whispered and disappeared towards the front of the house.

The two flyers stood waiting in the pitch darkness, listening to the approaching horses. In a couples of minutes Scrubby was back.

" A dozen of 'em, I reckon," he informed them. " Coming up from the direction of the river. We're cut off on that side. I guess some smartie must have seen that durned torch."

" We'd better get out of here, anyway," said Clintock. " If they have seen a light this'll be the first place they'll come to. We could get some cover against the face of the cliff."

They scrambled out by the same window by which they had entered.

" Run straight for it, partners," said Scrubby as soon as all three were safely outside, " thar ain't time to take cover, and anyways I don't reckon they cin see us."

He himself led the way in a wild dash for the face of the scarp. They had covered half the distance when he caught at Clintock's arm.

" Hold hard, partner; listen!"

He cocked his ear in the direction of the horses.

" Tain't no use," he panted, " thar's a couple

of 'em coming right along the bottom of the cliff.''
Clintock himself could now pick out the individual clatter of hooves away to their left.

'' They must have spread out,'' he said.

'' Sure. I might hev guessed they would. Thar's
nothin' for it, partners, we'll hev to skip back and
take cover round them tanks. Maybe there we can
slip through the cordon.''

Clintock nodded.

'' Come on, then.''

He led the way across to where, in the gloom,
they could pick out the long, low blobs of dark
shade that, from the top of the scarp, they had seen
were tanks.

'' Spread out, pards,'' Scrubby whispered from
behind, '' we'll stand a better chance each man on
his own. We cin rendezvous beside the river where
we camped at sundown.''

'' O.K.,'' Clintock whispered, and himself made
for the furthest tank.

There were five of these reservoirs, each some
two hundred feet long and forty wide. They spread
out in a line southwards from the bottom of the
cliff and parallel to it.

'' Don't retreat no further,'' Clintock caught
Scrubby's parting caution, '' else we're pinned
'tween them and the other river.''

The oncoming cordon of horsemen had practically reached the building they had just left when
Clintock made the western end of the far tank and
crouched there to get his breath.

Across the plain he could see, above the distant tangle of jungle, a semi-circle of yellow light. For the moment he was at a loss to account for this phenomenon; then he realised that more time than they had thought must have slipped away while they were examining the contents of the safe. The two hours that Scrubby had counted on had elapsed, and the moon was rising.

He half saw, half heard, the leading riders rein in in front of the building which they now knew was da Cuyta's headquarters. Across the still plain he clearly heard the shout of an order, the words of which he could not catch. The two riders by the house dismounted. Evidently the whole troop was acting on some prearranged plan, for the rest of the cordon came to a standstill. The silence, broken only by the occasional stamp of a horse, was worse than the menacing thunder of galloping hooves.

For a moment or two Clintock toyed with the idea of breaking cover to the south and making a wide detour to round the flank of the Indians and thus strike eastwards till he reached the river, which he could then follow up to the rendezvous Scrubby had suggested. But a moment's thought revealed that a leader sufficiently wily to cut off their escape along the face of the scarp would also have covered his other flank.

He stared southwards, straining his eyes for the sight of any movement. After a minute or so he heard the jingle of a bridle as a horse twitched its mane. The sound enabled him to pick out the shape of a horseman about three hundred yards away, almost due south of him. The Indians evidently planned to do exactly what Scrubby had feared—drive them from the cover of the buildings and pin them in on the west river, where they would be forced to choose between surrender or a grisly fate in the water.

The search of the headquarters was evidently finished, for the two riders emerged and remounted. Another order was shouted, and the cordon moved forward some twenty yards.

In the growing light Clintock could now distinguish two more horsemen covering the back of the buildings.

Minutes passed while the second house in the line was submitted to the same thorough search, only to culminate in the same relentless move forward when the search proved fruitless. Clintock cast a desperate glance to the south again. The outrider on his flank had moved in, and now sat motionless in his saddle, a bare hundred and fifty yards away.

A stir among the horsemen round the buildings recalled his gaze to the oncoming cordon. Some one shouted, and a man who was evidently the leader galloped up. Clintock crossed over to the other side of the tank to get a better view.

One of the horsemen was holding out for the others to see some object that his keen eyes had picked out lying on the ground. They were

examining this carefully. Presently one of them
held it against the light of the moon, now hanging
like a lantern on the eastern sky. For a split second
Clintock caught its silhouette. It was Scrubby's
hat.

The discovery occasioned a few moments' conference among the Indians. Clintock racked his
brain for a stroke which might turn this respite to
their advantage, but could think of none. To
move, except with the greatest care, was dangerous, for he feared the keen ears of the outrider to
the south of him. To break cover would be tanta-
mount to suicide in the strengthening moonlight.
And yet to stay where he was meant inevitable discovery as the cordon of horsemen concluded their
work.

The clatter of hooves to the east focused his
attention in that direction once more. The horsemen had broken their line, and now formed a circle
round the third and larger building which Scrubby
had surmised was some sort of refinery. Evidently
the discovery of the hat had led them to believe that
the fugitives had taken cover in this building.

This time four of the horsemen dismounted and
entered the building. From this closer range Clintock could almost follow their movements as they
lit lamps inside and, occasionally shouting to one
another, ransacked the place from end to end.

His flesh crept as he saw the men emerge. Their
leader mounted and, with one brief order, pointed
to the line of tanks, the only remaining cover.

Clintock yanked the revolver from his belt, but before he had time to take aim there came the crack of a shot from the left of him. Evidently Scrubby had opened fire, and to some effect, for the leading horseman came crashing to the ground.

Crack! Crack! Crack! Scrubby sent bullet after bullet whistling down the avenue between the two tanks, and another rider flung up his arms and slipped sideways off his horse.

" Now, partners," he heard Scrubby's cheerful voice ring out, " run up the far side as the critturs come through the centre—an' try to git a horse."

It was then that the full subtlety of Scrubby's desperate manœuvre dawned on Clintock. The Indians, enraged by the shooting, flung their previous careful position aside. Breaking the cordon they rode in a bunch straight down between the two tanks from which the shots had come, leaving the ground on each side uncovered. There was just a wild hope of dashing up the far side of the tanks, grabbing a horse from one of the fallen riders and getting a start away to the east.

Clintock leapt out and ran full tilt down the long side of the tank. But he had reckoned without the rider to the south. Hardly had he broken cover than he heard the thudding of hooves. Something sang through the air behind him, and a weight caught him sharply on the shin. He came down like a pole-axed steer. Quickly he made to scramble to his feet again, but his legs were trapped, enmeshed in a bolas: a spider's web of rope, each

end weighted with an iron bolt. A moment later
the Indian who had thrown it jumped off his horse
beside him and held the point of a knife at his
throat.

For a moment they stayed thus poised. Then the
Indian, with a quick jerk, took his revolver and
thrust it in his own belt.

From across the tanks came a shout, and the
fellow who had captured him answered. Clintock
listened, hoping to hear the sound of horses galloping away to the east, but all was silent. Evidently
his companions had shared his own fate.

The Indian stood back and motioned to Clintock
to get up. The latter, grateful to be relieved of the
painfully suggestive prick of the cold steel on his
gullet, unwound the bolas from his legs and
scrambled to his feet.

Almost before he realised what was happening
the Indian dropped a noose of rope round him,
pinning his arms to his body. The end of this the
Indian fastened up short to the horse's bridle, and
thus bound he led the flyer away.

As far as he could judge, for he dare not turn for
fear of stumbling, Clintock reckoned he led the
procession of captives and captors southward
across the plain.

Presently they slithered down a dip on to one of
the points of the great star design, and he soon
realised that their immediate object was the building in the centre.

His curiosity almost overcoming his apprehension, Clintock saw in the moonlight as they approached that this was of the same gigantic blocks of stone as all the other buildings at Ithi Caru.

As they reached the threshold of a great doorway on the north side, the Indian dismounted and ignoring his prisoner, prostrated himself on the ground. Then he rose and, unhitching the rope, led Clintock inside the door.

The inside of the temple, for so it had the appearance, consisted of three concentric walls of stone, each more massive than the first, and so pierced with doorways that no two openings were opposite each other.

They descended a steep slope to the second wall. The whole building seemed filled with a growing roar as of water rushing through a narrow space. Passing through this wall, they crossed, still descending, to the third one, in the thickness of which were rooms.

The Indian stopped and again prostrated himself. Then, treading reverently, he led Clintock through the third archway.

The scene that was revealed took the flyer's breath away. The third wall enclosed an amphitheatre some seventy yards across, from the circumference of which great tiers of rock descended to an arena about forty feet below, and in its centre there rose ten feet of tearing, roaring flame, filling the place with its light and sound.

A sharp tug on the rope brought Clintock back

to reality. He was led round the amphitheatre to
a doorway on the far side, which revealed that
this, the south quarter of the temple, was divided
up into chambers fitted between the sweep of the
encircling walls.

Into the largest of these he was taken, the rest
of the cortegé filing in behind. At the far end, on
a kind of dais, sat an elderly bearded Indian of
magnificent stature, and beside him da Cuyta.

" All highest," the leader of the Indians stepped
forward and waved a hand to his prisoners, " here
are the men."

" You fool!" da Cuyta leaped to his feet.
" these are not the two! Who is this man?"

Clintock turned for the first time and saw that
he pointed to Scrubby, who stood, bound simi-
larly to himself, a few feet behind. And with a
sudden leap of hope he realised that Dandy was
not there.

CHAPTER TWENTY

IT ALL DEPENDS ON DANDY

WHEN, led by Scrubby, the three of them had made their first dash for the face of the scarp, Dandy had lagged behind his two companions.

Ahead of him he had heard rather than seen Scrubby stop Clintock, and hearing his suggestion to cut back to the oil tanks, Dandy had slewed round sharply to make off in that direction.

In doing so he caught his foot in a crevice in the hard rock and fell heavily. Quickly he scrambled to his feet and went to follow the others. But his first stride brought him to a limping standstill, dragging a twisted ankle.

For a moment he stood in the darkness, uncertain what to do. To call out would invite discovery—worse. Burdened by a limping man, their chances of escape, even if Scrubby and Clintock reached him first, would be *nil*. With characteristic philosophy, he lay flat down in the nearest pocket of ground and decided to leave the rest to chance.

Fortune favoured him. The riders had anticipated that the fugitives would either stay in the cover of the building or else dash along the face of the cliff. The men between the two had eyes only for the buildings that were being searched, expecting any minute to see their quarry make a final run for liberty. One Indian, indeed, reined his horse in a bare thirty feet from him, but after a grim five minutes, the cordon moved forward, and he realised they had passed over him.

Even so he had little hope of escape. To move would spell disaster, to stay where he was merely delayed the issue till daybreak.

When, a quarter of an hour later, he heard the shots and Scrubby's shout, he was half persuaded to make a dash away. But the possibility of jeopardising the chances of the others deterred him.

Not being aware that the Indians were only looking for two men, the complete withdrawal of the search party, after the capture of his companions, nonplussed him. Sitting up, he watched the retreating horsemen, scratching his cropped thatch in amazement.

" Well," he thought to himself, " if I am the last man free, it's up to me to do something."

In default of any definite plan he set off back towards the east river, with some vague idea in the back of his mind that if he could get back to the valley where the cache of stores lay, he might gain a respite to rest his leg, and perhaps concoct a plan of future action.

But his ankle irked him terribly. Each step on the hard rock racked him with agony.

" Blast!" he muttered to himself, " I hope it's not broken."

Gritting his teeth, he struggled on, half limping,

half hopping, and so after nearly two hours he came upon the river. In utter exhaustion he flung himself down on the bank, and lay for some minutes half unconscious.

The thunder of galloping hooves away to the south roused his flagging energies. Now that the moon was up he could make out a troop of horsemen going at high speed along the great rock roadway that ran northwards from the temple in the centre of the plain. It flashed across his mind, and in this he was right, that somehow the Indians must have found out that he had escaped.

He cudgelled his brains for a new way out. As soon as the Indians had again searched the buildings against the cliff, he realised, they would for certain trail him eastwards. Even granted that the search gave him an hour's grace, he could not hope to get away across the top of the scarp and back to the broken country on the western side of the plain.

His gaze wandered eastwards across the river to the matto on the other side. There he would be safe, at least for the time being. Acting on the spur of the moment, he waded into the vile smelling water and struck out for the far bank.

But the Rio de Vinagre, as Scrubby had dubbed it, was a very different proposition from its sister on the other side of the plain. Wider and stronger, its rapid current caught him and swung him away southward. He realised before he had been in the water a minute that his three mile limp away from

da Cuyta's headquarters had exhausted him more
that he had imagined. The water too, stung his
eyes to a point of blindness, and caught at his nose
and throat.

Turning on his back he floated, sucking great
gulps of fresh air. In this fashion he managed to
keep himself afloat with the minimum of effort,
and afford some respite to his aching limbs.

" At any rate," he consoled himself, " nobody
would ever dream of a bloke doing this."

He lost all sense of the time he had been in the
water. Only the dull ache of his ankle prevented
him from going into a drowse. With a jerk, he regained a grip on himself.

" No you don't," he addressed himself aloud,
" You stick the thing out. Come on, you blighter,
swim."

He turned over and again struck out for the
opposite bank, but the current was too strong for
him. Gradually a new danger dawned on him.
One bank or the other he must make, for if he got
swept below the confluence of the two rivers he
might lose contact with Ithi Caru for good.

He fell to scheming again. If he could get right
down to the Indian City in the confluence, he might
get a chance of some sort of a boat. Once across
the west river he could, with any luck, make his
way back to Scrubby's original camp.

The creation of a definite plan of action had re-
vitalising effect on his mind. He started swimming
again, this time with the object of keeping himself

in towards the right bank. Even this lesser task
proved difficult and by the time he had succeeded
in working back across the current to within a few
feet of the bank, the appearance of a wall warned
him that he had reached his first objective.

Ahead in the gloom he picked out a flight of stone
steps running out from the bank into the water.
With a supreme effort he cut across the last feet of
swirling torrent and a few seconds later he
dragged himself out and lay gasping across the
bottom two steps.

Judging himself to be momentarily safe, Dandy
rested himself thoroughly before starting on the
next stage of his plan. He decided his best chance
lay in breaking into a nearby house, and stealing
some dry clothes, in which he would be less conspicuous than in his dripping overalls.

It was about half an hour later, therefore, that
he mounted the steps and took a cautious survey
of the land.

His first impressions were favourable. The
Indian city was much greater in extent than he had
previously imagined. The tumble of houses and
huts spread for fully two miles along each of the
rivers. But the only lights were in the buildings
themselves. The narrow stretches of bare ground
between these were deep in shadow. At a distance
he could hear voices and movement, but the part
in which he stood seemed deserted.

At a limping run, he made the nearest wall.
Some six feet high, it was the bounding wall of the

courtyard to a big house alongside the river. With a jump he heaved himself astride the crest of it. From his position he surveyed the near side of the house. All was in darkness.

" This looks promising," he told himself, and lowered himself gingerly to the ground to avoid landing on his injured foot.

Keeping in the shadow of the wall, he made his way across the courtyard. The windows, like those of the buildings in the north of the plain, were mere apertures, but these were covered by heavy hangings.

He climbed in and took stock of the fair-sized room in which he found himself. Even by the moonlight he could see that it was much better equipped than any he had seen since the start of his adventures in Brazil.

With his back to the window, he pondered. In a civilised room you know where to look for clothes; there are chests of drawers, cupboards and the like; but here, as far as he could make out, there were none. He had just decided that this must be a living room, rather than a sleeping room, when his speculations were rudely interrupted by the sound of footsteps.

He turned and swept aside the hangings to climb through the window. But even as he did so, he realised that it was too late: The footsteps were in the room, which evidently had no door. To disturb the window hangings would call attention to himself. He stayed as he was between the window and hangings, and prayed that these latter reached the floor.

Whoever had come into the room was apparently not alarmed, for he heard the footsteps going backwards and forwards as one might in the darkness in familiar suroundings. A moment later came the scrape of a match, and light appeared on the far side of the hangings. He tensed himself to strike, for now, if at all, he faced discovery. The footsteps came nearer, and he sensed that a bare two feet separated him from the person in the room.

Suddenly the hangings were swept aside and he found himself face to face with Alison.

Almost before he fully realised who his adversary was he had leapt clear of the curtains, and pinned her by the throat against the wall.

She made no attempt to struggle, but just stood there, eyes shut, body rigid, her face very pale.

Followed deadlock. After a moment's pause Dandy released his hold and stood back.

" What—" he said nonplussed, " what's the matter?"

Alison opened her eyes and they were full of wonder.

" I thought you were going to kill me," she said simply.

Dandy took rapid stock of the situation. Nobody else was yet aware of his presence in the Indian city. Only this slip of a girl stood between him and a fair chance of escape. His own life was unquestionably at stake, and the only remaining hope of Clintock and Scrubby. To the men Alison was in the habit of dealing with, he knew, the only course of action would be logical, but he knew as deeply as he realised his dangers that he could never bring himself to do it.

He smiled wryly.

" I'm sorry to disappoint," he said, " but I'm afraid I couldn't."

They stood for a long minute staring at each other. Then Alison asked:

" What are you going to do?"

" I don't know," Dandy told her, " and that's a fact. Why the devil did it have to be you?"

He started to walk across to a chair to sit down, but his ankle gave under him at his first step and he had to hop the rest.

" Oh!" said Alison, " you're hurt."

" It's nothing. Just twisted my ankle running away from your pals."

" I can bind that up," she said. " I know how."

And she fetched a length of cloth, knelt and took off his shoe, and bound his ankle tightly.

" You know," said Dandy, looking down on the Titian head bowed over his injured foot, " this is so ridiculous I could laugh if it wasn't for fear of offending you. Here I am, in the middle of a hornet's nest; whichever way I turn there's a bloke waiting to put a bullet into me, and you're carefully bandaging my sprained ankle. You ask me what am I going to do. The whole question is, what are you going to do?"

She knotted the bandage and stood up. The deep brown eyes took stock of him with an intenseness that made him blush to the roots of his hair.

" You gave me my life to-night," said Alison slowly, " and once before. I cannot take yours. You must stay here."

CHAPTER TWENTY-ONE

AFTER the Indians had gone da Cuyta rang a hand bell at his side.

Out of the darkness round the walls there glided a wooden-faced orderly. Da Cuyta rapped out a command in Quanchi, and the orderly left as silently as he had appeared.

" And so." Da Cuyta leaned forward with a sneer. " We meet again, Squadron-Leader Clintock."

Clintock met his gaze squarely.

" It looks like it," he said calmly.

" But this time you have another friend—eh?"

An ironic smile broke the thin line of Clintock's lips.

" Forgive me," he bowed in mock politeness, " I forgot to do the honours. This is Senhor Boulder."

" Boulder?" Da Cuyta glanced sharply at imperturbable Scrubby. " I think I have heard that name before?"

" Yeah?" drawled its owner laconically. "We're a pretty big family, not to mention the Dam. That was named after my uncle Abraham."

Da Cuyta's reply was curtailed by a movement at the far end of the hall. Into the ring of light cast by the torches stepped the tall, erect man who had flown with Lieutenant Gomez. He crossed over to da Cuyta and the two held a whispered conversation. Finally a point was put to the bearded Indian who had sat, meanwhile, as immovable as a statue.

The result of the conference was that the questioning of the prisoners was continued by the tall man.

" Where is the man you came here with?" he asked Clintock, speaking in English, with a thick rasping accent.

" Gone."

" Gone? I am not joking, Clintock, I want to know; and if you won't tell me of your own free will, I shall find means to make you."

" You seem to know my name," Clintock sidetracked. " What's yours?"

" My name?" The tall man drew himself up. " My name is Colonel Gutliev. It's a pity you have never heard of me, it might persuade you to talk quicker."

Clintock shrugged his shoulders.

" As to the vileness of your reputation, Colonel, I don't doubt it. But as far as Flight-Lieutenant Paget is concerned, I can't tell you where he is, because I don't know and nor does my friend, Mr. Boulder."

Clintock saw the Colonel's face change and he scrutinised Scrubby.

" Boulder?" he mused. " Step out here, you."

" Why certainly," Scrubby complied. Then he

said lightly, " Looks like some member of my family's been round here sellin' something."

" Where did you come from?" The Colonel grasped him by the arm.

" Steady, partner." Scrubby's voice was soothing. "Thar ain't no need for violence. I bin around this country for years."

" Then what are you doing with this man?"

" Why as to that, partner," Scrubby lied easily, " I ain't with him, leastways not until to-day. I fetched up with him way north there this afternoon. Said he was looking for his pal, and I slung along of him fer reasons that this is a mighty lonely country."

" And so you came down here. Why?"

" Why?" repeated Scrubby. " Waal, partner, this guy reckoned his pal might be this way, and I didn't see no harm in heving a look round the point. Kinda oil strike you got here—huh?"

The Colonel laughed, a thin, mirthless laugh, nearer to a sneer than anything else.

" It is, Mr. Boulder," he said, " as you will find out in good time, perhaps."

He turned again to Clintock.

" If what this man says is true," he said, " you haven't seen Paget since this afternoon?"

Clintock had an inspiration.

" I haven't seen Paget since yesterday," he said. " We got separated after the General's men so kindly drove us into the river. For all I know he may be dead."

Gutliev surveyed the pair of them. " So," he commented, " you are determined to lie."

" Me?" answered Scrubby, " not me, partner. I went to Sunday School."

" You've made a very pretty story," Gutliev sneered, " but I'm afraid it doesn't pass, gentlemen. There is just one little snag. When our aeroplane from Lower Valley passed over you up on the top there, the pilot distinctly saw Paget there. It so happened they spotted you and got a pair of glasses on him before you took cover. The pilot,"—his voice took on an oily leer—" the pilot remembered Paget very well. What do you say to that?"

" I don't," Clintock countered, " but if you saw Paget, as you say, why were your men only looking for two of us?"

It was a subtle trap, but Clintock's quick brain had seen the flaw in it. Gutliev turned on his heel and returned to the dais, where he again consulted da Cuyta in undertones.

Presently he turned again to the prisoners.

" You force me to be unnecessarily brutal "— he shrugged his shoulders. " But before we get on to that I want to tell you what we propose doing with you, just in case you are not in a fit state to appreciate it afterwards. You, Squadron-Leader, are going to join our cause——"

" I won't," Clintock interrupted him, " you can smash me to little bits before I lend a hand in your dirty business."

Gutliev nodded gently.

" Exactly," he said. " That is what we are going to do. But not to little bits, because then you wouldn't be recognisable, that is most important. I don't know how far you gentlemen are aware of our general plans, but for purposes which need not concern you we intend to take advantage of a critical situation between this country and the Argentine Republic."

" Really? That's news to me." It occurred to Clintock that in the unlikely event of his getting out of Ithi Caru alive, the more he knew about da Cuyta's plans, the better.

" We have arranged it." Gutliev dismissed the matter with a shrug. " But at present we are faced with the problem of convincing ten million surprised Porteños that their government is the victim of a foreign plot."

" That shouldn't be difficult, since it's true."

Gutliev treated them to another sneering laugh.

" Ah," he corrected, " but intervention is foreign to us. The hand we have in this will only be apparent later."

" Too later, I guess," interposed Scrubby grimly.

Gutliev transferred the sneer from Clintock to him.

" Your humour, Mr. Boulder, is excellent. I hope it lasts." He returned to Clintock. " But to continue we propose to overcome the natural reluctance of both countries to take the first steps;

we are going to take the first step for them—an air-raid. The actual choice of objective will be decided by our agents back east, but among the casualties on our side will be—yourself."

Clintock gritted his teeth in impotent fury.

" So simple, isn't it?" Gutliev went on smoothly. " We had originally planned to fake it, and leave the rest to propaganda; but your so convenient arrival saves all that. Not only does everybody know who you are, and your official position, but imagine the interpretation we can put on your flight. Believe me, Squadron-Leader, I'm grateful to you."

" I don't know what you hope to gain from that," said Clintock.

" Gain?" Gutliev feigned surprised. " My young friend, you disappoint me. I'll tell you what we shall gain. Confusion in the south; support for the non-intervention party in the United States; and deadlock in Europe. It will last a week, perhaps, this sad state of affairs. By that time we shall be virtually masters of Brazil, and then the indignant denials and the detailed refusals won't matter. We shall be established as the champions of freedom in Latin America—simple isn't it, Squadron-Leader?"

Clintock bit his lip. He realised only too well that what Gutliev had foretold would come about. Before he could say anything Gutliev turned to Scrubby.

" And you, too, Mr. Boulder. You will be very

useful to us. It means that we shall be able to save Flight-Lieutenant Paget to go with his friend. Perhaps you would care to come to the doorway?"

They followed the Colonel across the hall to the doorway, and stood gazing down on the amphitheatre with its tearing pillar of flame.

"Impressive—isn't it?" Gutliev rubbed his hands enthusiastically. "Just a jet of natural gas, and the Indians built their temple round it. They call this place Ithi Caru. I believe it's a corruption of the Indian for "Bride of the Sun." According to their legends this plain was once so beautiful that the sun itself fell in love with it. And one day at high summer he rushed down from the heavens to embrace its beauty. The result of the embrace was this dry, scorched plain, and in the centre the offspring of the sun. When the sun saw this, apparently it was overcome with remorse. The Indian for oil is 'Tears of the Sun.' I trust you follow me, Mr. Boulder?"

"Yeah," drawled Scrubby, "I hev to, my hands are tied."

"Every year"—Gutliev ignored the jibe— "the sun climbs higher from the northern horizon and passes the zenith. When it has dipped a little to the south it returns again to the zenith. The Indians celebrate it as the Feast of the Return. They believe that unless a sacrifice is made to the sun on that day he would next year sink farther and farther to the south and eventually pass below the southern horizon for ever."

He pointed to where, beside the vent in the rock surface from which the flame sprang, a platform of stones rose a yard above the rest of the arena.

" They place the victim on that stone, and soak him in oil. At a given signal the stone is tipped. I am told it's a remarkable sight, and the ceremony is very impressive. For the most part the sacrifice is usually a horse, or some wild animal, but this year we need something particularly stimulating for our Indian troops before the great march of re-conquest commences. They will settle the west, while we deal with the east. So we are going to revive the ancient custom of human sacrifice. You, Mr. Boulder, will have the privilege of being the central figure. I hope you appreciate the honour?"

Scrubby stared blankly at the leaping flame.

" When," he asked at length, " when does the breakfast come off?"

" The day after to-morrow," Gutliev told him.

He paused to allow his words to sink in. But if he hoped for any reaction to show in Scrubby, he was disappointed. The little Virginian calmly turned his back on the arena and grinned at Clintock.

" And now," Gutliev turned to Clintock, " we must go into the question of Paget again."

He held up for the airman's inspection a small brass instrument some four inches in height, consisting of two bars and a screw by which anything placed between the bars might be crushed.

" Quite a genuine antique," commented Gutliev. " A real Spanish thumb-screw, Squadron-Leader. Have you ever seen one before?"

Clintock did not answer.

Gutliev shrugged his shoulders and made a sign to the two soldiers who had followed the prisoners from the hall. They grasped Clintock on either side and pinned him between them.

But the airman made no effort to resist. Calmly he held raised his left forearm to Gutliev.

" Carry on," he said.

Gutliev raised an eyebrow. He stared at Clintock. " You seem very ready," he said.

He stood in thought while Clintock faced him.

" No," he said at length, " it is just possible when they find you that some honest man will see the marks of my little toy. They would deduce that you were flying under compulsion. A little damning to your personal honour, but it will spoil the effect."

He rapped out a command to the Indians, who released Clintock and pinioned Scrubby instead.

" On you, my friend," Gutliev fixed the thumb-screw in position, " the marks will not show. Now, do you refuse to tell me where Paget is?"

Neither prisoner answered. Exerting all the weight of his powerful shoulders, Gutliev gave the screw half a turn. Scrubby grimaced. The sweat started up in drops from his temples and trickled down his face.

" Where is Paget?" demanded Gutliev.

Still stubborn silence. Gutliev's eyes alight with the joy of his work, applied himself to the screw again. Under its tan, Scrubby's sturdy face turned ashen. He ground his teeth. Twice again Gutliev applied himself to his work, wrenching the screw home into the crushed flesh. Scarlet suffused the dull polish of the instrument and great, sullen drops splashed on the stones.

" You swine!" burst out Clintock, writhing in his bonds.

Gutliev turned to him and sent him reeling against the wall with a back-hand blow.

" Tell me where Paget is, or keep your mouth shut," he blazed. Clintock subsided. A man with his arms bound to his side is helpless as a new-born babe.

Still Scrubby stood firm, his veins standing out like whipcords, his head thrust forwards as though under a great burden. Panting with his own exertions, Gutliev stood back to allow the agony to rack his victim to the full.

" Where—" he demanded—" where is Paget?"

Still no reply from the bowed head. Again the Colonel heaved at the screw with all his strength. Scrubby shuddered as though a sudden fever had seized him, gradually he sagged forward like a man half asleep. His legs gave under him. The Indians released their hold and the gallant little Virginian collapsed to the floor like an empty sack.

Then, and then only, as consciousness left him, did a moan break from his lips.

CHAPTER TWENTY-TWO

"THE INDIANS ARE COMING!"

FOR DANDY the next twenty-four hours was a nightmare. He passed the night on the floor wrapped in a pair of coarse blankets that Alison had given him. His ankle ached abominably, and the stone floor was not a soft mattress. Turning and tossing he spent the hours now dozing, now racking his brains for some definite line of action for the morrow.

Just after dawn it started to rain. The heavens opened and solid sheets of water came drenching down, lashing at the house like a wild animal. Across the river he could hear the trees groaning and soughing in the wind.

He got up, for he could no longer bear to stay still, and examined his ankle. He found that the bandage had prevented the worst of the swelling, and he could move it freely, though with great pain. He hopped across to his clothes, which he had stretched out to dry. They were still slightly damp, but quite wearable and he struggled into them.

While he was still undecided on his next course of action, he ate half the food Alison had left for him the night before. Then he took stock of his position.

He came to the conclusion it was impossible to move before nightfall. Nothing was to be gained by taking colossal chances in the daylight, and getting captured himself. In the meantime he must do something about his foot.

He had little medical knowledge, but his common sense told him that the quickest cure lay in exercising the bruised muscles

Setting his teeth he started gingerly to limp up and down the room. Twice his exercise was interrupted by movements in the house, but no one came near him.

Gradually his foot responded to the stimulation, and he managed to get his heel to the ground. Resolved to take no half measures Dandy kept grimly on, while the rain came down outside as though flung by an indignant hand.

Resting every hour, as he judged, he kept on the go till midday. Then, exhausted by his pacing, he sat down and ate the rest of his food. The wind had dropped and the rain now fell in a straight curtain. The heat of the day was worsened rather than relieved by the damp, and across the courtyard came curling the dank, cloying smell of the river and the matto beyond.

He settled himself on the floor, his back against the wall. His foot throbbed but no longer gave him pain. Gradually the monotonous tattoo of rain on the stones outside lulled him, and drugged by the heat and his own tiredness, he fell asleep.

He woke to the familiar sound of marching feet;

gradually the steady tramp forced its way into his consciousness and he started up.

The rain had stopped, and the night was heavy and still. Nothing moved around him except the steady tramp, tramp of men on the far side of the house. His heart quickened as mentally he judged the number of men that must be passing. He listened in the dead silence. In civilised countries the march of troops is usually accompanied by the acclaim of crowds, by trumpet and drum, or the singing and joking of the troops themselves. But in this Indian city not a sound stirred but the unending tramp of men.

After what seemed an age, the sound of marching died away, only to be replaced by that of another vast body of troops moving in the distance in another direction.

His curiosity roused beyond caution, Dandy ran from the room and searching through the house he found his way to the roof. Above the walls of the house ran ramparts, between which stretched the peculiar, crude roofing which characterised all the buildings at Ithi Caru.

From the corner of the ramparts, Dandy could see clean across the roofs of the city. Southward, near the point of the confluence of the rivers, the tumble of buildings gave way to a magnificent square. Straining his eyes he could make out on the far side a raised terrace, lit by scores of flaring torches. Drawn up on every side of the terrace stood rank upon rank of men, blurred in the distance into a solid, dark mass.

Of the figures on the terrace he could see nothing, but as he watched, fascinated, there stepped into the torchlight the slim figure of a girl. It was Alison.

Across the still night he heard the treble of her voice, raised in exhortation. She spoke with a magnetism that he could sense even from the distance. Her hands straight beside her, she used none of the clowning gesture of the modern demagogue, but under the lash of her voice he felt the silent masses before her ripple with emotion.

Nothing he had ever seen matched the effect of that still white figure in the torchlight; the rise and fall of that clear, high voice, and silent ranks of wooden-faced soldiers.

Suddenly her speech reached a climax. She flung her arms upwards and remained poised, her face upturned to the heavens. Across the countless ranks there rose and swelled a thunder of deep voices repeating a prayer.

Dandy turned from the sight bewildered, and seized with a sense of impotence. If only he had Peter; Peter with his knowledge of the country and the language; Peter with a reason for everything.

His injured foot forgotten, he stumbled down into the house again. Losing his direction he blundered into a different room from the one he had left. He felt round to try and identify it. His hands fell across the familiar shape of a radio set. Half in desperation, half in curiosity, he turned the power switch, and found to his surprise that the set was working.

Gently across the night came the tones of a dance tune. He realised by the waves of fading in the reception that it was coming from a great distance. Entranced with a sudden sense of unity with the world he had lost, he sat on a large chest beside the set and listened. Suddenly the music faded, and he heard the voice of an announcer:

" This is the National Broadcasting Alliance of Chicago, interrupting our dance hour to bring to you the up-to-the-minute news from the world's latest storm centre.

" There is still no reply to the Brazilian Ultimatum, given yesterday to Argentine. If no satisfactory reply comes before midnight to-morrow, local time, the northern Republic has reserved the right to take whatever action the preservation of her rights and interests requires. No certain indication is given of what form this action may take.

" Hope of peaceful settlement rose to-day when it was learned that the President's appeal to both states not to call up army reserves found unexpected support in Rio de Janeiro.

" Meanwhile the dispute has occasioned unprecedented outbreaks of violence throughout Latin America.

" Here are to-day's news snapshots from the American Continent:

" BOLIVIA. In La Paz students paraded and, carrying banners calling on the government to resist United States vassalage, marched on the Legislature. The crowd was not dispersed until the police opened fire, killing seven and wounding thirty.

" CHILE. In Valparaiso the extreme United People's Party issued a manifesto laying the blame for the threat of war on Britain.

" ' Great Britain,' it says, ' will welcome this opportunity of strengthening the grip, lost in the European War, on her Argentine food supplies, for none can doubt that virtual annexation will follow any military steps, taken under pretext of protection against an external foe of Britain's own creation.'

" UNITED STATES. In Washington, Senator Donkelly, commenting on the despatch southward of U.S. warships *Wyoming* and *Arkansas*, together with four destroyers and two escort vessels, said to-day: ' The United States can best protect the interests of her nationals by conserving her strength, not flying hither and thither in panic. War has taken place in Latin America before now without threat to our integrity!'

" JAMAICA. To-day's report from London speaks of the situation as quiet. The troops landed yesterday in Kingston are stated to have the situation in hand. Normal communications will be resumed with the island to-morrow.

" From the island itself comes an unconfirmed report of the beating to death of a white assistant by the workers on one of the up-country sugar estates.

" AND FROM EUROPE. Two cruisers of the British Navy, *Sheffield* and *Glasgow*, left Gibraltar to-day and steamed westward. No official statement was made on their destination, but a correspondent on the Rock speaks of a probable rendezvous with the South Atlantic Squadron off St. Paul's Rocks.

" In conclusion, National Broadcasting Alliance proudly repeats to its listeners the President's message to the nation of this morning. ' There is no call for alarm. The United States Government is watching affairs to the south and this government is neither unprepared nor weak!'

" If there is any further news to-night on the general situation, N.B.A. will bring it to you. Stay listening."

The announcer's voice faded and the dance music was resumed. In his mind's eye Dandy pictured the dancers saying to each other, in the security of three thousand miles of land and ocean, " How terrible, those poor creatures down there."

And he, Dandy Paget, was sitting alone, unarmed and bewildered in the hub of the whole maelstrom. His thoughts were interrupted by the return of Alison. He hurried down to meet her.

She turned as he came into the room in which he had spent the day.

"Oh!" she said, "you're here. Where have you been?"

"Up on the roof," he said, and he realised she was panting as though she had been running.

"The roof?" She moved away from him in the gloom. "Then you saw——"

"Yes. Whose are those troops, Alison? What are they doing here?"

"Doing here?" She uttered a little silver laugh. "Nothing, here. To-morrow they will march, then there will be action."

"March?" asked Dandy, still grappling with the meaning of what he had seen, "march where?"

"One division goes southward"—her voice took on the fanatic edge that had impressed him so at Lower Valley—"into Bolivia; the second eastward across the mountains; and the third down the rivers to Manaos. While we are raising the standard of freedom in the east, they will surge onwards, down the rivers, through the mountain passes. Suddenly across the fat, lazy cities the word will fly 'The Indians are coming.'"

"No!" Dandy broke out, "you can't let such a thing happen. Think of the horrors you are turning loose on innocent people. Think of mothers crowding their children round them in fear; of whole villages trudging away from them in terror."

"No one will be hurt unless they resist," said Alison. "If they resist, they must be ground to the dust before the march of freedom. To-morrow is a new era in the history of the world."

Dandy stood dumbfounded. He realised that nothing he could say or do would change the girl from her views.

"I must go." Alison came near to him, and spoke in her own quiet voice. "You will be safe after to-morrow."

She pressed his arm, and ran out of the house. For a moment Dandy stood wondering. Then resolution seized him. He ran up again to the room where the radio set was.

More important things even than Peter and Scrubby were at stake now. Across the west river somewhere was Boulder's horse. With that a desperate man might make the nearest settlement in time to warn the whole countryside. But he must have some disguise to get through the Indian city.

With this in mind he flung open the chest he had sat on to listen to the broadcast.

Quickly he turned out the contents, examining each by the faint light from the dials of the radio.

The top layers were all blankets of the same coarse texture as those in which he had slept. Below he came upon a broad-brimmed hat, and a pair of bombachas.

CHAPTER TWENTY-THREE

ALISON LEARNS THE TRUTH

As soon as Clintock heard the door slam behind them, he knelt down to tend the stricken man, thankful that they had cut his bonds and hustled him into the same chamber as the one into which, choking with impotent fury, he had watched the Indians drag the little Virginian's inert body.

He lifted Scrubby's arm, and the unconscious man groaned pitifully. Clintock made a fierce resolution—If indeed, he was to pass into the shadows, then given half a chance, Gutliev should die also.

He realised that in the few hurried hours he had known Scrubby, there had grown between them a bond of respect and friendship, such as only men who have suffered together know.

The mangled thumb hung limply across Scrubby's corny palm. Feeling in his pocket Clintock produced the only apparatus he had to make a splint—a pencil and his own soiled handkerchief. His movement of the hand and arm had started the wound bleeding again, with such rapidity that this, he saw, must be his first concern.

Quickly he broke an inch of the top of the pencil and laid it along inside of the wrist; round this he

bound the handkerchief and knotted it as tightly
as he could, to make a tourniquet on the radial
artery. Almost immediately his efforts were re-
warded by a marked lessening of the flow of blood.

Using the rest of the pencil, and strips from his
own shirt, he padded the injured thumb and bound
it as near as he could judge in a natural position.
He settled Scrubby as comfortably as circum-
stances allowed.

Daylight came before sleep found Clintock himself. With the dawn he feared a new visitation of
Gutliev, but evidently the Colonel was too busy
elsewhere.

He decided that the best thing he could do was
rest. If by a miracle a chance of escape came, it
would not be until they were taken from the cell,
and then the more refreshed he was, the better.

Towards midday Scrubby's occasional moans
ceased and, crossing over to examine his prostrate
companion, Clintock realised that the coma had
passed and Scrubby was in a deep, natural sleep.

During the afternoon he heard the sound of
engines above the steady drumming of the rain.
The room in which they lay faced eastwards, and
Clintock craned his neck to the one tiny aperture
that served as a window. Presently he was re-
warded with the sight of two flights of six planes.
Just for an instant he saw them climbing into the
lowering sky, and then they were lost in a flurry
of cloud and driving rain.

Towards nightfall the rain eased up, and he

heard a great stir and commotion in the temple. He waited, expecting any minute to see the door open and Gutliev swagger in followed by half a dozen Indians. But no one came near them, and after dark a deep silence enfolded the temple and the whole plain.

It was late at night when Scrubby woke. Clintock in a half daze, heard his voice.

" Are you there, partner?"

The airman went over and knelt beside him.

" Yes, Scrubby, I'm here. How do you feel?"

" Not too bad. They gave me a rough run, partner."

He went to sit up, inadvertently pressing his injured hand on the floor, and collapsing with a stifled cry of agony. Clintock lifted him gently and supported his head and shoulder against his knee.

" I'm sorry, Scrubby," he said, hardly trusting his own voice, " it ought to have been me."

" Nary a bit," said Scrubby, and for all the weakness of his voice it carried the old indomitable spirit. Then he asked anxiously :

" They didn't get Dandy, son?"

" No," Clintock told him. " I've been listening all day; there'd been a commotion round here if they'd caught him, but nothing's happened."

" Good," Scrubby nodded. " Then it wasn't wasted. He's a good kid that Dandy, he'll make out."

"You bet," said Clintock with a good deal more confidence than he felt.

He turned quickly for beyond the huge bronze-faced door he had caught the sound of footsteps.

"Who's this?" whispered Scrubby.

"Nobody, I dare say," said Clintock with a forced cheerfulness. "I've heard the same sort of thing several times while you've been asleep."

But a moment later the door swung ajar and an Indian slid in carrying a lamp. He motioned to Clintock to stay still, and whispered a few words to somebody outside. A moment later a figure heavily shrouded in an Indian blanket slipped in. The Indian retired, and they heard the door clang to. The figure dropped the edge of the blanket from its face. It was Alison.

"You?" gasped Clintock in amazement. Gently he propped Scrubby against the wall and stood up to face the girl. "What have you come here for?"

"To save you," said Alison quickly. "If you will only do what I say, there is still time."

"What do you want me to do?" Clintock asked dubiously.

"Join us." The brown eyes were full of earnest appeal. "Da Cuyta is short of pilots. I know; I have heard him say it, and you are more skilled than any we have. If you will fly for him he will spare your life and your friend's."

"Oh, no, he wouldn't," said Clintock. "He wouldn't trust me, in the first place."

Alison waved his objection aside.

" He will do it if I ask," she said impatiently. " You will be watched, of course, but as long as you carry out your orders you will be safe."

Clintock turned away. For himself he had no concern, but the lives of two other men were at stake.

At length he turned again to Alison and spoke to her gently.

" Don't misunderstand me," he said. " I'm grateful. You must have risked a great deal to come here and try to help us. Only——"

" Only what?" she broke across his words. " Make no mistake. They will do what they have threatened. Even now it will be difficult. By dawn it will be impossible to save you."

" I know," said Clintock solemnly, " but some time ago I took an oath of allegiance. I didn't think much of it then—few of us do—but there are times when it comes back to a fellow very forcibly. This is one of them."

In the silence that ensued he heard Scrubby say beneath his breath:

" Thank God! "

" And in any case," Clintock went on, " I would die a hundred times over rather than lend a hand in your business."

" Why?" asked Alison, and in her voice he recognised genuine resentment. " Ours is not a mean cause. What makes you hate us so?"

" I admire you!" said Clintock quietly. " As

to your friends—to me they are nothing but a crowd of gangsters trying to grab power for themselves by fair means or foul.''

'' No,'' cried Alison, '' that is not true. If we have shed blood it was because it was necessary. To-morrow we are setting out on a crusade—nothing less. In every city in this continent the Flag of Liberty will be raised. We are not fighting for an empire of greed and oppression, we are fighting for freedom: to create the empire that Bolivar dreamed of, the empire he gave his life to. Bolivar stirred a glorious flood of heroism here in America, a flood that your countrymen turned into the filthy channels of commercialism. Led by you, Americans have turned against each other, fought and wasted their golden heritage, instead of living in it, as was their right. Just as the Spaniards stripped the gold from the temples of the Incas, so Britain has sucked the mighty wealth from the fields and mountains of this land. And after Britain was gorged to the full, the United States, snaring our statesmen with promises of money, twisting every natural failing to their own advantage to fill their own fat paunches. And meanwhile the peons starve in mud huts, and no American can look at his country and call it his own! And you, you who spring from the race who were the authors of all this misery, you call us gangsters.''

The flood of oratory staggered Clintock. He had never seen a girl so beside herself with the passion of her own beliefs. "I made no criticism of your objects," he turned the trend of the dispute. "Your methods are enough for me."

"Methods?"

"You forget." Clintock held her by the very contrast of his quiet, earnest voice. "I went into the cellar at Lower Valley."

"That is nothing," she said, but he could see her wild flood of enthusiasm had faltered; "nothing that has not been done elsewhere scores of times."

For answer Clintock put another question.

"You know my friend, Paget," he said. "Would you call him a coward?"

"I think he is the bravest man I have ever seen."

The intensity of her tones surprised him. Quickly he went on:

"You are right. But I'll tell you something, Alison, something that Dandy has never breathed to a living soul except me, who was his friend almost before he could talk. Dandy has a secret fear. Sometimes at night he dreams about it, and wakes soaked in sweat.

"I will not believe he fears anything," the girl said fiercely.

"He does," Clintock told her. "He fears that some day he may be ordered to take an aeroplane and go and drop bombs—bombs like those stored at Lower Valley—on helpless women and children. Don't misunderstand me. It isn't the thought that he might be shot down. If Dandy were ordered to fly a thousand miles across country packed with enemies he would climb into the cockpit with a smile. It's the thought of the horror he might one day be forced to bring, not to soldiers, for that he would accept as inevitable, but to mothers and old men, to children not old enough to understand, to little babies squalling in their cradles till their voices go hoarse with fear. He told me once that if he were ordered to carry out an expedition of intimidation bombing he would shoot himself."

She recoiled before his words.

" We don't intend to do that," she protested.

" You do," said Clintock. " You know it as well as I do. Those bombs at Lower Valley are intended to break the spirit of any one brave enough to resist you."

Alison nodded. " That is true," she admited, " but you can see for yourself, if you think, that it is the most merciful way. We are bound to be misunderstood. There are always people who will obey their governments blindly. And that way is the quickest way. To press home the iron will shorten the agony."

" Who told you that?" demanded Clintock. " Answer me "—he seized the girl by the shoulders—" who told you that? Gutliev?"

Alison nodded. In all her life she had never seen any one so terrifying as this tall, dark

English boy with his piercing eyes and his quiet voice.

"So Gutliev told you!" Clintock relaxed his grip. "He has duped you like the rest of them. That argument has been used to justify every atrocity ever committed, Alison, and it has never been true. Do you suppose that nowhere, except in your ranks, there is a brave man? Don't you see that you cannot reckon on the thoughts of thousands of people as though they were so many ciphers in a mathematical problem? Your simultaneous uprising will only half succeed. Here somebody will be afraid at the last moment, there somebody will make a mistake, or you will be betrayed. Some of your risings will be put down, and the forces against you will be as strong as ever."

"No," said Alison with all a fanatic's conviction, "the plan is ready to the last detail. Colonel Gutliev himself prepared it."

Clintock attacked from another angle.

"And from what country in South America does the Colonel come?"

Alison paused, and Clintock saw he had scored another point.

"He doesn't," he answered his own question. "Colonel Gutliev is one of a body of foreign experts who have nobly lent their services to General da Cuyta, isn't he?"

"Yes," said Alison defiantly. "You don't

suppose we lack sympathisers in the outside world, do you?''

'' I'm sure you don't,'' Clintock agreed. '' But isn't Colonel Gutliev taking rather a strong hand for an adviser? Gutliev hurried your plans, didn't he? The plans he himself had drafted. Gutliev questioned us last night and decided what was to be done with us. If I had agreed to help you, your greatest difficulty would have been to persuade da Cuyta to override Gutliev, wouldn't it?''

He saw that his chance shot had gone home.

'' We have accepted his help,'' said Alison. '' We owe him a great deal.''

'' Yes,'' returned Clintock, '' but not as much as you are paying. It is for Gutliev that the blow must be quick and merciless, it is for Gutliev that blood must be shed, that a political movement must be turned into an army.''

'' Our outside support only makes our victory the more certain,'' Alison insisted.

'' Does it?'' mocked Clintock. '' Gutliev told you that too, didn't he? Do you suppose that his is the only country that will interest itself in your struggle? What he can do for you others can do for those who will oppose you. Would you turn South America into another Spain, Alison?''

'' You are mistaken. Gutliev is merely one factor in our organisation.''

'' Is he?'' asked Clintock. '' Tell me, Alison, how many pilots have you persuaded to desert and come up here?'' The girl started in surprise.

" Oh, don't be so sensitive. I know everything about that little game. Answer me, how many?"

" About twenty," she said.

" Twenty," repeated Clintock, " and da Cuyta has two hundred 'planes."

" He hasn't," burst out Alison.

" He has," Clintock countered. " You go and look at the map in his office. There are sixty here, alone. And where are the pilots coming from? From Gutliev? And all the arms you have and your ammunition? There isn't an arsenal in South America capable of supplying them, so who will? Gutliev! He may have started as an adviser, but he has the whiphand now. And what will be the result? Your magnificent crusade will end in a bitter, dreary struggle. Everybody who might have sympathised will hate you, you will be forced to desperate moves, the cost of which will fall on you, and not on the real people who made them. And then, when you have won your hollow victory, what will you have? Not that glorious Empire of Freedom you were raving about. In all the world you will only have one friend to lean on—Gutliev. Then you will see such a reign of terror and expropriation as you have never dreamed of. All carried out beneath the shadow of your Banner of Liberty. Pizarro's plunder of Peru, our exploitation, will pale beside what Gutliev and his friends will take in return for their part in your rising. And you—you will not dare to refuse, because you are a puppet. That is

Gutliev's game. He is using da Cuyta's ambition just as da Cuyta used your own ideals—to his own gain. And you will put American liberty back for a century."

Alison stood, her hands clenched, her eyes blazing.

"If I thought that," she said fiercely, "I would kill Gutliev to-night."

"And get a worse man, if that is possible, in his place to-morrow. No, Alison, your only chance of saving Brazil and all America is to get us away from here."

"Oh!" Alison turned on him as though he had struck her. "You have shown your true colour. You are lying to me to save your own skin."

"Was I so concerned about my own skin when you offered to save it?" asked Clintock.

The girl hesitated. Clintock fished in his inner pocket and produced the sheet of cipher he had taken from da Cuyta's safe.

"Read that," he ordered, "and judge whether I am lying."

Alison took the paper. He saw that her hands were trembling as she scanned its contents.

"It is a fake," she cried in indignant disbelief.

Clintock shrugged his shoulders.

"If I were you," he said, "I'd take it to Gutliev and ask for an explanation. It may cost you your life, but——"

Alison stared at him. She turned slowly and studied the line of pencilled Portuguese.

" Da Cuyta's—eh?" asked Clintock.

Once again his luck held.

" It is," she said, and her voice had the flat, dead tones of a person who has been tricked.

" It is his."

Clintock waited. For a full minute Alison stood staring, fascinated, at the tell-tale paper as though it were a snake. Then, with a cry like a stricken animal, she turned from him, wrenched open the door and fled into the night.

Clintock leapt after her, but the Indian outside was quicker. The door slammed home as he reached it, and he heard the bars rasp across on the far side.

CHAPTER TWENTY-FOUR

DANDY LOOKS FOR A WAY

THE MOON was just rising as Dandy emerged from the house in which he had spent the last twenty-four hours. He turned out from the chest a pair of knee-length chirapas, the common form of nether garment in the Matto Grosso, and a striped shirt. He carried a blanket, Indian-style, over his shoulders, and had smothered his face with the red clay drift that formed the only soil on the plain. In the stark daylight he knew he would cut a ridiculous figure, but in the half-shadow of the Indian city he looked less conspicuous at a casual glance than in his overalls, betrayed even in the darkness by the white of his face.

While he had thus attempted to disguise himself he debated his best course of action. To strike northwards along the Rio de Vinagre had the advantage of comparative safety, but entailed the twenty-mile circuit of the whole plain, even if he found some ready way of negotiating the ravine with its wrecked bridge. It would then be daylight before he could hope to find Scrubby's horse, and he would have lost many valuable hours. He had resolved that his only chance of getting away with sufficient start to do any good was to strike straight across to the west river. If an army was to move the next day there must be transport of some description somewhere. He pinned his hopes on the chance discovery of a boat or other means of crossing the piranha-infested water.

There was nobody in his immediate vicinity as he dodged quickly over to the shadow of the nearest row of huts, but from every side came the sound of life and movement. He pressed on and crossed over the first intersecting street. Negotiating it brought him in view of a group of Indians standing some fifty yards away. His heart hammering, he stepped out boldly into the moonlight expecting every moment to hear a shout hailing him, but none came.

Turning to his right, he made for the fringe of the city, thinking that there he stood less chance of meeting anybody, only to shrink back into the nearest alcove as he heard the tramp of an approaching body of troops.

To his dismay he realised that they were coming straight down the street in which he now stood. To turn and run, his first impulse, would be asking for trouble; he squirmed himself back flat against the wall and hoped for the best.

The troops came on; at their head there swaggered a man who was evidently their officer. He wore a limp, army cap cocked at a jaunty angle and carried himself with a swashbuckling air. His uniform consisted of a bright blue shirt, a pair of close-cut velvet trousers of some dark material, and heavy riding boots. Across his shoulders and round his waist he carried a miniature arsenal, and in his hand a short riding whip. As he passed, Dandy caught to his amazement the familiar words:

" I love the dear fingers so toilworn for me.
God bless you and keep you, Mother
    Macree."

The voice had the easy, insolent brogue that has carried the Irishman triumphantly the world over.

Then came the troops. Three abreast, they marched superbly. Dark-skinned men, in whose impassive, almost Mongolian faces only their eyes lived. There was no attempt at uniform in their dress; every man different, they wore the odd assortment of clothes that men collect in a country where life is casual and supplies of any manufactured article haphazard.

But every one of them carried a bandolier and a rifle. If there were no uniforms in da Cuyta's army, there was no lack of equipment; and the discipline was of an order that is beyond the understanding of civilised man, where mass courage is a thing to be nursed by every device known. They marched in silence in perfect formation, each man an automaton, accustomed all his life to no other direction than the decrees of his priest-ruler. Dandy judged there were fully four hundred of them in this one company, but he saw no other Europeans.

This then was da Cuyta's infantry. He had re-discovered the born soldiers that the Incas had wielded, and officered them by every reliable desperado he could buy into his service in the up-country provinces, where the disappearance of a man here and there is hardly a matter for the most casual comment. Men who all their lives had lived by desperate makeshift, who would have to obey him because, once having committed them-selves to his service, would find no other refuge in the American continent. And into the hands of such captains and thousands of Indians who knew no fear of God or man, he had somehow contrived to put the weapons of civilisation.

As soon as the last file had faded into the dark-ness he hurried on. Growing bolder as he passed block after block of buildings without exciting suspicion, he nearly ruined his own chances by walking straight into a small square thronged with Indians.

In the centre a space had been cleared by the crowd round two Indian women who manipulated with savage intensity a couple of instruments, a cross between a violin and a mandolin. Beside them squatted a bag of skin and bones in human form beating with equal frenzy a small leg drum, which he gripped between his knees. The music had a queer, throbbing rhythm that sent the hair creeping on the back of Dandy's neck.

Strung across the open space half a dozen couples were performing a dance. The onlookers followed them with their eyes by the light of a couple of flaring torches, beating, the meanwhile, the music's rhythm on their own thighs. The music and the dance held the crowd like a drug.

Dandy turned again and plunged into a cross-wise alley, the music drumming in his ears. To him it seemed to symbolise the savage intensity of the forces that da Cuyta was about to launch against the helpless population of the surrounding countries. He shuddered, and broke into a run, not stopping until the music had faded into the general hum of the city.

Everywhere he turned he saw signs of preparation for the great march on the morrow. In one corner he ran across a group of men sharpening hundreds of knives on a huge grindstone wetted with the blood of a chicken, the dripping carcass of which was squeezed above the stone by a gloating crone. It was with a sense of tremendous relief that he broke clear of the last houses and found himself facing the empty plain.

He breathed deeply the warm night breeze, and with a conscious effort he dismissed the feeling of the hopelessness of his task which the sights in the Indian city had impressed on him. He had made no plans of his movements after his immediate escape, and as he turned his footsteps westwards towards the river he tried desperately to fill this gap in his programme, but without any great success. In the end he consoled himself with the thought that if he could get to any town with a telephone he might get in touch with the nearest British consul. But it was with little comfort that he remembered he had left in his overall what little money he had brought with him on the flight.

He passed nobody in his three-mile walk, and gradually his spirits revived. Somewhere there would be a way.

As he approached the river he trod more cautiously, for to his left he could hear the sound of shouts and voices. He closed in on the nearest buildings and approaching the water-front stuck his head round to see what was happening.

Half a mile down the stream, to his delight, he saw a cluster of heavy rafts, each some thirty feet square, drawn up against the bank. But in the same moment his hopes were dashed, for the rafts were swarming with men, who, under direction from the bank, were evidently rigging a pontoon bridge across the river. Amongst them the chances of passing unnoticed were *nil*, for the men would probably be all of one company and well known to each other. And even if he managed by some lucky chance to get away with one of the rafts, it would be physically impossible to manœuvre the clumsy craft across the current single-handed.

To his right stretched the line of long, narrow buildings following the sweep of river which da

Cuyta used to house his air force. They seemed deserted.

With some desperate idea of getting away with a 'plane, half-thinking that farther up the river he might find some small boat, but chiefly because there seemed nothing else to do, Dandy started northward up the line of hangars.

But it seemed that da Cuyta was taking no chances. The massive door to the first building was firmly shut. From the distance he scanned the flat stretch of river bank in the moonlight, but there was no sign of a boat.

Nothing daunted he kept on up the line of hangars, examining each in turn, but without result. In the end he fetched up at the same hangar in which he and Clintock had found themselves when they landed at Ithi Caru.

He stood gazing across the moonlit plain, and once again he would have given his ears for Peter's guidance. Racking his brain, the only idea that came to him was of finding some material to fire the 'planes, and with this in view he was in act of weighing up the possibilities of carrying some oil from the distant tanks to the hangars when his attention was caught by the clatter of hooves.

Coming down the great black roadway which stretched in the moonlight like an arrow almost from his feet to the distant temple was a single rider.

He drew back into the shadow of the hangar and waited. The horseman came thundering on, and he saw by another cautious glance that the horse was being viciously spurred.

He stayed crouched against the wall, wondering if there was a chance of unhorsing this lone rider and thus getting away to the north.

With the hoof-beats barely a hundred yards away the horse was reined in, and came the rest of the distance at a walk. Passing between the first two hangars, the horseman came to a stop and sat, apparently scanning the ground between the hangars and the river. Once more himself, now that he had a task that was more suited to his mind, Dandy crept like the Indian he had disguised himself to be along the shadow to the far end of the hangar and out across the forty feet that still separated him from the back of his unsuspecting quarry.

But he had scarcely covered half the distance when a cry of amazement broke from him. In the moonlight he recognised the rider as Alison.

And in the same moment he realised that she was sobbing.

CHAPTER TWENTY-FIVE

AWAITING DEATH

Dawn found Clintock still awake. He stood at the window watching, as the light strengthened, for the first pink streamer on the eastern horizon. Gradually he saw the different colours of the landscape gather contrast; the grey of the plain, the dirty white of the sky, and, between the two, the black band of the distant Matto. Almost as soon as he had picked these things out, the tangled line of jungle was thrown into silhouette by the rosy forerunners of the dawn. A minute or two later the edge of the sun itself lifted in a halo of blood-red mist.

Within the temple behind him he heard the deep notes of a huge gong booming out every half minute. And then the drums started. Never in his life had he felt the menace of a sound so much. They carried the hollow timbre of the jungle war-drum, and across the plain he heard an answering tattoo from the Indian city.

He shuddered, despite himself, and turned to Scrubby.

" Make some noise, don't they," he remarked.

Scrubby nodded.

" Anything worth seeing out of the window?" he asked, for with his shorter stature he could not reach the narrow aperture. Clintock answered with a shake of his head.

An hour passed. Only the incessant throb of the drums broke the silence in the cell. Each man was deep in his own thoughts. Only once did any exchange of words take place.

" I hope Dandy got away," said Clintock.

" Me too," assented Scrubby. " I liked that kid."

" How's your thumb?" asked Clintock.

" Blamed sore." Followed a long pause. " It doesn't matter much, I guess."

And they both relapsed into silence.

The approach of the troops brought their attention to the window again. Gradually, under the maddening rhythm of the temple drums, they heard the sludge-slidge, sludge-slidge of marching feet.

Clintock looked out and whistled softly to himself; then he hoisted Scrubby up to see. Passing from the Indian city in an unending stream round towards the north entrance of the temple was a column of men, three abreast.

" The audience arrives," commented Scrubby dryly.

" What time," queried Clintock, " what time d'you think the ceremony will start?"

" Depends," said Scrubby, " but I don't figure my part of the proceedings will come before noon. These Injun religions are all based on positions of the sun."

They fell to silence again; the troops passed on.

" Must be a terrific number of them," said Clintock when he could bear the silence no longer. " They've been going past for close on an hour."

" 'Bout fifteen thousand, I guess," Scrubby opined, " and still more to come."

" I wonder how they managed to get the arms for them right up here?" mused Clintock.

" Oh, easy enough. You kin get a fair-sized vessel right up to these parts from the Atlantic," Scrubby told him. " Middle of the last century they surveyed for an inter-oceanic canal, but it didn't go on. Panama killed it, I guess. But you said about the arms. A power of stuff came up this way during the Bolivian war with Paraguay, and I'm thinkin' a right sizable proportion never reached the Gran Chaco."

Clintock nodded.

" It's just that," Scrubby went on, " that'll make these critturs different. For years they've been oppressed, though they form eighty per cent. of the population in these parts. 'Twas a matter of arms, you see. Ef the Injuns got uppish, why they just called up the troops and shot 'em down like cattle. Down thar in Sante Fé I met an Argentine captain who boasted he'd killed more Injuns than the average guy had flies. Retired he was, mark you. They haven't had a real set-to with their Injuns hereabouts for forty years."

" I've heard about the Indian troubles when I

was a nipper," said Clintock. "Even then they were old men's stories."

Scrubby nodded.

"The Dons smashed up all their organisation. The Jesuits took away their religion and thar wasn't what you might call a civil life. The religion was the government and vice-versa. They hevn't had a leader above a village cacique for centuries. But up here they seem to have kept a bit of the old Empire goin' and I reckon when da Cuyta found this joint he just rubbed his hands in joy. Fer it gives him just the binding force he wanted. The Injuns knows no loyalty to any country or any government. Why, half the critturs don't even know thar is a country or a government."

"But he won't find it so easy with his officers," said Clintock. "Not if he really means to carry out this plan of uniting the whole continent that Alison raves about."

"Why as to that," said Scrubby, "I daresay the Injuns have their own leaders; and the rest were never born in the southern hemisphere, I'll lay a dime to my uncle Abraham."

"He's got some Brazilian pilots," objected Clintock.

"A few," said Scrubby, "an' maybe one or two others from Chile or Peru, but you pointed out yourself where the rest came from."

Clintock nodded.

"I wouldn't be surprised if this isn't a fusion

of two schemes," he said. "Da Cuyta planned a conquest on land, Gutliev from the air. Neither would work by itself. Da Cuyta's would be too slow; Gutliev's impossible because he had no means of real control. And one day the two schemers happened to meet."

The marching of the troops passed at last.

"I don't like to think of that lot loose in countries where the standing army couldn't count on more than eight or nine thousand men, probably not so well equipped." remarked Clintock.

"Nor I, partner," Scrubby agreed. "Ain't a pleasant prospect."

They heard the bars on the door grating across. Clintock stood up.

"This looks like us," he said. "A bit before we expected."

The two men faced each other in silence for a moment, then Clintock held out his hand.

"Good-bye, Scrubby."

"Good-bye, partner."

"Yes," said Clintock, and somewhere in his heart he found a laugh, "we were partners, weren't we? Good partners."

They clasped hands.

A moment later a dozen Indians rushed into the cell and grasped the two men. Evidently they expected their victims to struggle, for they pinned the prisoners quickly and bound their hands to their sides. The leading Indian motioned to them to move forward.

"We're to be together a bit longer anyway," said Clintock as they left their prison, and were led away towards the centre of the temple.

They passed through the second and inner walls and found themselves half-way down the tiers which led to the amphitheatre. On every side, filling the tiers to the roof, the vast building swarmed with Indians, every man armed to the teeth.

A deep shout rumbled across the massed soldiers as Scrubby appeared. Every man raised his hands and the thunder of a prayer echoed round the walls. From somewhere behind them rung out the brazen tones of the gong that had greeted the rising sun.

But they were not led, as they had expected, down into the arena where the flame leaped and roared. Instead, in an intense silence, their guards led them across the open space at the south quarter of the temple towards a doorway decorated with every conceivable turn and twist of burnished artistry.

Half-way across, the guards halted them in front of a line of men, evidently the Indian leaders, for they prostrated themselves before proceeding. In the centre of the line Clintock, who was first, picked out the figures of da Cuyta and Gutliev dressed in a braided green uniform. Of Alison there was no sign, and it struck him that in all that concourse there was not a single woman.

He passed the General and his adviser without

turning, but Scrubby halted in front of Gutliev. The two stood eyeing each other at a distance of three feet. Suddenly, without a word, Scrubby spat with the velocity of a toad, catching Gutliev clean across the face.

The tall man started forward with a raised hand but evidently this was the last thing desirable, for da Cuyta held him back and a moment later he controlled himself.

As silently as he had offered the insult Scrubby turned and marched on, a contented grin playing with the corners of his mouth.

" I'll go easier now," he said to Clintock as they passed through the doorway into a room built into the thickness of the inner wall of the temple.

Clintock waited till the door swung to, shutting out the view of the crowded temple, then he said:

" That did me good, Scrubby. I wish I'd thought of it."

" What d'you make of this place?" asked Scrubby.

" Sort of vestry, I suppose," said Clintock.

The room had no windows, nor was there the slightest vestige of furniture or ornament. It was hot as a furnace.

They stood and waited.

CHAPTER TWENTY-SIX

THE END OF ITHI CARU

PRESENTLY they heard a multitude of voices raised in some sort of hymn from within the temple. Below them came the thud, thud of wood on stone.

"They can't have any machinery here, surely?" said Clintock, as the regular thudding continued. "What is it?"

"Don't ask me," began Scrubby, then suddenly he stiffened and stood staring at the corner of the room. Clintock followed his gaze, and felt his scalp creep as he saw a solid block of stone in the corner tilt. The thudding was renewed. The block tilted still further, and in the space revealed came a small hand, followed by a head, and a moment later Alison scrambled out of the floor.

"Quickly," she whispered as she slashed at their bonds. "Bring the ends of rope with you, we must leave no trace."

They needed no second bidding. Four or five feet below the level of the floor was a platform of rock on to which they scrambled, heaving the stone block back to a horizontal position.

"I hoped they would bring you in there before the sacrifice," said Alison, breathlessly. "It was our only chance, and then I was terrified I wouldn't be able to shift the stone."

They descended a flight of steps and found in a niche at the bottom a lighted lamp.

This Alison took and led the way forward. Their path sloped away rapidly, and as it became cooler a faint, cloying smell reached out to them. They gazed in wonder at the sight the flickering lamp revealed, for the tunnel was hewn from the solid rock that formed the plain.

" It is the Indian burial sanctuary," Alison whispered. " Those places "—she indicated one of a series of narrow bays cut in the wall of the tunnel—" are called the Houses of the Dead. They're crowded with corpses."

Scrubby sniffed.

" I was in a mortuary once at Sucre," he remarked pointedly. " 'Twas worse than this joint by far."

" They embalm their dead," said Alison. " You will see."

The tunnel levelled out and led on and on, its floor thick with a fine drift of dust, which muffled their footfalls.

Clintock judged they had come over a mile when the tunnel opened out sharply into a hall, a hundred feet long and forty high.

" Look," said Alison. " Have you ever seen a sight to equal it!"

She held the lamp above her head and in its widened radius of light they could dimly make out a huge statue which filled the centre of the hall.

It was of a man locked in mortal struggle with a

gigantic bat, the wingspread of which must have been forty feet. The carving was so perfect that they could almost fancy it moved. Around the man's head, thrown back in the effort of forcing down the colossal vampire, radiated a series of spikes, and as the lamp guttered they caught the sparkle of countless gems. The figure of the man glowed redly in the fitful light and Clintock realised it was of gold, and his assailant was worked in that jet black rock that also formed the roadways centering on the temple.

" The sun and darkness," Alison explained in an awed tone, " struggling for mastery over the world. Come closer."

She led them to the foot of the statue and held the lamp for them to see what they had taken for a series of minor figures.

Around the statue, witnesses of the eternal struggle it depicted, there sat in golden thrones a line of kings. Dressed in richly embroidered robes, they sat, erect and crowned, and as the fugitives gazed they realised that these were no statues, but the perfectly preserved bodies of the ancient priests of Ithi Caru.

" Come," urged Alison, " there is no time to waste."

At the far end of the Hall of Death they found the tunnel led out again, and they pressed on. It seemed to Clintock that they must be plunging into the very bowels of the earth, for fully an hour had passed since they left the temple.

At length Alison halted.

" Stay here," she whispered, and they saw her pass up a similar flight of steps to those that led down from the temple.

Daylight flashed and disappeared somewhere above them, and they stood facing each other in the lamplight.

" What's the time, partner?" asked Scrubby suddenly.

Clintock looked at his watch. He had wound it regularly since the day he had set it by calculation at Lower Valley. The hands pointed to twenty minutes to two. He made a rough calculation.

" Just on one, I should think."

" I figured it must be," said Scrubby anxiously. " I reckon back there it's getting precious near the time for my solo turn. I wish that gal would hurry."

As though to point his words there came echoing far away down the tunnel the pad, pad, pad of running feet.

Scrubby dowsed the lamp, and they scrambled for the stairs in the inky darkness. Clintock went up first and climbed till his hands touched a ceiling above his head; putting his shoulder to it he shoved. The rock did not budge. Desperately he shifted his position about a foot and shoved again. Still no result; behind him, the footsteps in the tunnel were appreciably nearer.

A third time he strained his muscles against the

rock above and almost went sprawling as it yielded easily.

He heaved himself through and, turning, caught Scrubby's hand and lifted the little Virginian bodily up to ground level. They pushed the stone block back into position and looked around them. In the gloom of the building in which they found themselves Clintock recognised the shape of an aeroplane. They were in one of the huge hangars by the western river of the plain.

" This way," he ordered and doubled towards the northern end, where a shaft of daylight indicated the door. As he reached it he ran full tilt into Alison.

" Quick," she gasped. " They have missed you. They're coming across the plain."

They dashed out into the sunlight. A couple of hundred yards from the hangars were drawn up in a single row, stretching from end to end of the line of buildings, forty or fifty 'planes, the sun dancing on their glistening wings and fuselages. Beyond, streaming from the distant temple, came a veritable flood of Indians running like madmen.

" That one," shouted Alison, and pointed to where, behind the rest of the machines, a huge, low-winged monoplane stood. As they ran for it the twin-engines leaped to life, and the 'plane shifted a little for her wheels were not blocked. The door to the cabin hung open, and they clambered in, Alison fetching up breathless in the rear. In the pilot's seat sat a man in the same green uniform as da Cuyta and Gutliev had worn.

"We're done," gasped Clintock, who had rushed forward with the original idea of himself taking the controls.

"Not on your life," said the green-uniformed pilot gaily.

He turned to grin at them. It was the round and cheerful face of Dandy Paget.

From out of the windows of the cabin as he stood breathlessly watching the plain go past at ever increasing speed, Clintock saw one lone rider who had spurred his horse out of the rest of the mob and ridden obliquely across the plain to head them off. He recognised that it was Gutliev by the carriage of his head.

The Colonel reined in the lathering horse and levelled the gun he carried at his saddle.

"Peter," yelled Dandy, "pick him off. He's going to put a bullet into our propellers."

Even as he spoke the Colonel fired twice in quick succession. The window of the cabin splintered like a living thing. Another shot—their starboard engine raced and whined like an animal in agony and the great 'plane lurched with the sudden disturbance of power.

At his feet Clintock saw a long, foreign rifle of the type that all da Cuyta's men had carried. He had it braced against the shattered frame of the window almost before the action had taken shape in his mind.

Beside him Dandy, white-faced, wrestled with the controls to nurse the lop-sided 'plane into the air. They came abreast of Gutliev at a range of barely two hundred yards. Both rifles cracked simultaneously and Clintock reeled back, but not before he saw Gutliev rise in his saddle like a puppet and slide crashing to the ground. In that moment the 'plane lifted clear of the earth. A hail of fire swept her from the Indians behind on the plain but the bullets flew wide.

" Are you hurt bad, partner?" Scrubby went up to Clintock.

" No," Clintock grinned, his teeth clenched. " He got me in the shoulder, that's all."

They watched the plain sink slowly beneath them. Suddenly Dandy shouted.

" The scarp, Peter! She'll never make it."

Dead ahead of them rose the three hundred foot face of the scarp that bounded the northern end of the plain of Ithi Caru. Clintock glanced down. Limping as the 'plane was with one engine out of action they had scarcely climbed a hundred feet. A wave of nausea seized him.

" I can't do it," Dandy shouted, nursing his stick, his eyes fixed on the wall of cliff a bare half-mile away. " She's loaded to the eyebrows, Peter!"

Clintock opened his eyes. For a bare split second he hesitated, then he flung himself forward into the nose of the 'plane where the bomb sights were, and felt beside them for the row of release levers. With a prayer he closed his hand over them and slipped them forward in one sweeping movement. A wave of relief swept over him as he felt the bottom of the plane press upwards as though a gigantic hand had lifted her from underneath.

" More, Peter, more!" He heard Dandy yelling.

He spread his fingers and felt one lever at the end of the row that was still upright. He slipped it forward and felt the 'plane lift slightly again. Through the bombing aperture he saw the edge of the cliff twisting slowly not fifteen feet below, and then the 'plane shuddered from stem to stern, as though the lifting hand had been replaced by a blow from a sledge-hammer. The machine went upwards rocking like a leaf, and the ground below seemed to expand into a gigantic maw and reach up at them.

Thrown from side to side by the lurching 'plane, he scrambled back, to find Dandy, pale but triumphant, pulling her level as a man might a bucking horse.

Scrubby touched his shoulder and pointed out of the window.

The machine had turned in its buffeting through a right angle and they were now flying eastwards. Below lay the sweep of the Rio de

Vinagre. But it was not at the river that Scrubby pointed.

Behind them he saw the spot on the cliff at the base of which the bombs had landed. The whole face of the scarp had come crumbling down like a pack of cards, and over the piles of splintered rock there came a gushing flood of black.

For a moment Clintock did not understand, then he realised that the force of the explosion had pierced the face of the cliff and released the titanic pressure of the oil it held.

Spellbound, they watched the black flood sweep southwards across the plain.

" The temple," gasped Scrubby. " Look!"

They saw the flood of oil go crashing against the outer walls, lap round the building and pass on. For a moment it seemed that nothing would happen, then there rose from the centre of the building a black tree; growing and spreading before their eyes it reached a height of two hundred feet and started to subside. Its centre was a tongue of dull red flame, and in an instant the whole plain was a sea of bellowing flame and smoke.

A second later they were all flung headlong as the force of the explosion hit the 'plane like a hurricane and for a second time that afternoon Dandy fought a life and death battle with the controls. Falling, Clintock struck his injured shoulder and the world slipped from him in a kaleidoscope of vivid lights.

When he recovered sufficiently to sit up they

were passing over the green carpet of the Matto Ahead the mighty Andes reared their white peaks along the distant horizon. Far behind, one spot in the Matto, dwarfed by the infinite expanse of never changing green, was marked by a smudge of black smoke.

CHAPTER TWENTY-SEVEN

" MEET THE COLONEL "

THE minutes ticked away into hours; silence fell on the occupants of the 'plane, and each made himself as comfortable as possible in the fuselage of the big bomber.

Dandy, an eye on the compass, steered due west on a magnetic course. For a chart they had only Scrubby's vague recollections of the South American continent. Corrections or tables they had not, nor any of the various instruments and data that form the foundation of accurate aerial navigation. Peter, nursing his injured shoulder, which Alison had roughly bandaged, stared moodily through the window, where the clamps and mounting waited in vain for the bomb-aimers' sight; below, the lofty crags of the Eastern Sierras of the Andes were already unfolding themselves in a long, straggling line of purply-grey stretching from horizon to horizon.

He looked up sharply as he felt a touch on his arm. It was Scrubby beckoning to him, and he clambered after the little American towards the tail of the 'plane, where the roar of the twin engines was dulled a little, and by dint of cupping one's hands and speaking right into the listener's ear it was possible to carry on a conversation of sorts.

"What's your idea of the next move?" Scrubby queried.

"I don't know. Carry on till we hit the coast and then turn north for Lima, I guess."

Scrubby made a dubious grimace.

"If we land on Lima airport with this tub it's going to take some explaining. You're supposed to be dead. I'm an unknown tramp, and Alison is probably wanted by every police force in South America. And we don't happen to own this 'plane."

"I doubt if anybody would care after we'd told them what happened at Ithi Caru," objected Peter.

"They'd never believe a word." Scrubby shook his head. "And we haven't a scrap of evidence, and there certainly won't be any at Ithi Caru. They'd be completely at sixes and sevens to know what to do with us, so they'd arrest us for sure, and once you're arrested in these troublesome times it isn't so easy to get out."

"O.K.," Peter nodded. "What do you suggest?"

"Land somewhere on the western foothills of the Andes or in an isolated valley. Burn the 'plane and make our way to the coast on foot. I've still got some money on me—have you?

"I think so." Peter felt in the inner pocket of his trousers. The contents of his wallet had suffered from repeated wettings and exposures, but the Brazilian money and, better still, his passport

were intact. "That suits me then. I'll tell
Dandy; you can explain to Alison."

Dandy, a little mystified at first at Peter's
shouts, finally nodded his agreement, especially
when Peter repeated the reference to Alison.

Half an hour later they were circling down
towards where, between two piles of rocky crags,
a green strip of verdure promised a fair landing.
Each, if they had any misgivings, watched in
silence while the valley below turned and rose as
Dandy nursed the big 'plane towards the earth.
Their luck was in—closer inspection revealed a
wide stretch of scrub and twists of grass half a
mile wide and four or five miles long. Peter gritted
his teeth and winced as the 'plane bumped and
shook his injured shoulder. For one wild minute
grass and sky and mountains flew past, then they
steadied, and came to a sudden, shuddering check
as a wing tip caught and pulled the big 'plane sideways and up on her nose.

"Out," ordered Dandy, who, as a precaution,
had kicked open the cockpit door in taxi-ing
across the improvised landing field. "Quick and
lively. Go on, Alison. Give Peter a hand,
Scrubby."

Within a few seconds all four were standing
beside the wreck of the 'plane.

"No more use to us now," grinned Scrubby,
who had retrieved the rifle from the bomber, and
taking aim carefully he put three bullets through
the petrol tank. As they scrambled back a tiny

flame licked out from the engine and, splitting, crept along the wing and back down the fuselage. A moment later a searing blast of hot air swept over them, and when, pausing for breath, they turned again the 'plane was an inferno from her nose to her tail-plane.

" Only an expert could sort that lot out," said Scrubby, as they stood with scraps of burning fabric and oil drifting down round them, " and I can't see anyone bothering to send one up here. Hallo!" he broke off abruptly at the sight of a horseman coming up the valley, " sooner than I thought. Now, listen, only you two were in this, and it was your own 'plane. Make up any forced landing story you like to cover the delay. Leave Alison to me."

The horseman, an Indian with a tremendous shawl and one of the huge multi-coloured hats so popular amongst the natives of Peru, readily accepted Scrubby's story that the Ingleses in their 'plane had crashed on and entirely destroyed his camp. A village, he informed them, was only seven miles away; he would ride in and get horses.

They arrived in the Indian village an hour later. The whole population, headed by the local chief, turned out to meet the flyers, and such hospitality as the meagre life of the Peruvian Indian permitted was placed at their disposal. Shortly afterwards the four of them thankfully lay down to get some badly-needed sleep.

It was morning when Clintock awoke. Beside

him Dandy lay snoring peacefully; of Scrubby
and Alison there was no sign. He scrambled out,
blinking, into the sunlight.

"Oh! the little señor and the lady," was the
reply to his question, "they left two hours ago."
The Indian eyed him with the candid stare of his
breed. "Did you expect him to wait? He said
you were strangers."

* * * * *

Three weeks later the Friends Abroad Club in
Lima gave a reception in honour of the two
English flyers, Squadron Leader Clintock and
Flight Lieutenant Paget, who had so unexpectedly
and miraculously completed their trip across the
South American continent. Peter had made a
good story for the press of the world: landing in
Central Brazil after having been struck by
lightning, he and his companion struggled several
days to make their machine airworthy, and finally
succeeded in taking off. This time, however, they
lost their bearings due to damaged instruments,
and, their petrol all but exhausted, they had
sought a landing on the western slopes of the
Andes; luck again deserted them; their 'plane
crashed in landing, caught fire, and became a
total wreck. They had completed their journey
by foot and horse.

As Scrubby had foreseen, none but a few stray
Indians ever went to see the twisted heap of
scarred metal in the centre of a patch of
blackened scrub, which alone could give the lie

o their story. Within a month the hardy mountain grass would come twisting through the tangled metal skeleton and hide it for ever.

On the day they left Ithi Caru there had indeed been abortive risings in one or two cities, but, shorn so mysteriously of its headquarters, da Cuyta's great organisation had become a mass of disjointed components, without force or direction. The risings passed without destruction and very little bloodshed. In South America a revolution, even if successful, will usually cause less disturbance than a general election in Britain or a Presidential campaign in the United States. The very internal troubles had served to settle the external ones. The Brazilian-Argentine dispute was off the front pages within a week.

These thoughts passed through Peter's mind as he sat down, amid applause, after replying to the address of welcome. On his right sat the president of the club and beyond that again Dandy was already making short work of his coffee and liqueurs. To Peter's left was a vacant seat.

" The Colonel's late," the president explained in reply to Peter's question as to the missing guest, " but he'll be along, I guess, any minute now."

But in that the president, shrewd Chicago business man that he was, fell in error. It was not till after the dinner was over and the guests withdrawn from the table that he approached

Clintock, cigar in one hand and glass in the other.

" Say, Clintock," he hailed, " come over and meet the Colonel!"

This belated dignitary had his back turned as Peter crossed the room. A short, powerful back, topped with a neat head of iron-grey hair that was somehow familiar.

" Colonel, I guess you've heard of our guest of honour——"

The Colonel turned. Gone was the beard, and when he spoke there was no southern hill-billy drawl, but the keen grey eyes were unmistakable. It was Scrubby.

" Clintock," went on the president, " meet Colonel Boulder, late of the U.S. Army. He hangs around here, just sort of hanging around. By the way, what *do* you get up to hereabouts, Colonel?"

The grey eyes twinkled.

" I'm delighted, Squadron Leader," Scrubby held out his hand in perfect calm to the gaping airman. " What do I do, Mr. President? Oh, I just sit about watching Uncle Sam's interests in a vague sort of way."

" I thought we paid consuls to do that."

" Why, so you do, Mr. President," the grey eyes twinkled even more merrily, " but you can't stop fighting men nosing their way into trouble sometimes, can you, Squadron Leader?"

" Er—no, I suppose not," Peter controlled

himself with an effort. He waited till the president, still carrying glass and cigar, had sailed off
to meet another latecomer.

" You're a sly customer, I must say," he
grinned to Scrubby, " why on earth didn't you
tell us the truth before?"

" Wouldn't have helped any," Boulder
shrugged his shoulders. " Thought I'd better let
you in the know now or else you might meet me in
Lima and let the cat out of the bag. Now you see
why I had to keep the whole affair quiet."

" How did you get to hear of it in the first
place?"

" Through the Indians; you'd be amazed how
rumour travels on this continent. Sometimes it's
fantastic, sometimes it isn't; it's always as well
for somebody to go and check up."

" What happened to Alison?" Clintock asked
suddenly after a pause. In his surprise he had
forgotten the fourth partner in their strange
adventure.

" She slipped off the very first night after we
reached Lima."

" I hope she gets on all right," Clintock said
dubiously.

" She will. That girl could make a niche for
herself anywhere in Latin America. She was
typical of the country itself; young, almost
childish in its desire for new things—new ideas,
new governments; brave to a point of lunacy over
many things that scarcely matter a halfpenny, yet